Looking *for the* Silver Lining

D.M. Bogacho

Quantum Discovery
A LITERARY AGENCY

ISBN
978-1-960197-27-6 (Paperback)
978-1-960197-28-3 (eBook)
978-1-960197-26-9 (Hardcover)

LOOKING *for the* *Silver Lining*

D.M. BOGACHO

Acknowledgments

William Shakespeare wrote, "I can no other ANSWER make but THANKS, and THANKS, and ever THANKS." My overwhelming gratitude goes out to all my sisters and friends who supported me and encouraged me during the writing of this book. Even though we were all going through something horrific, the 2020 Coronavirus Pandemic, everyone managed to give me the strength and fortitude to keep writing. A special thanks to my husband, Bob, for never complaining about the long hours of writing and for messing up our dining room table with my manuscripts, computer, and paper. Love to all!

REVIEWS

I thoroughly enjoyed this book. The characters were very believable and top notch. At the end of each chapter, it leaves you wanting to read more. I got totally involved in the character's lives and couldn't put it down. I read it in two days and I would highly recommend it!

BY HELEN BACKSTROM-TIBBETTS.

It takes a lot to "grab" my attention to get lost in a good book. I am happy to say that D. M. Bogacho accomplished just that at the onset. The story begins as a young woman of 18 searches for her dream in an unfamiliar country. However, what enfolds after embarking on her journey to America will make her see how her decisions will impact her life. Young and naive at first, Mackenzie Ables is a character that any one of us could relate to. Decisions that will change her as she lives through love, joy, deceit, intrigue, and heartache. Looking for the Silver Lining has you wondering what is coming next at every turn of the page. An easy read, but riveting!

BY JEANNE ELLIS

It took one turn of the page to become enthralled in Looking for the Silver Lining by D. M. Bogacho.

Mackenzie Ables' personality is what drew me in; she is filled with hope, she's spunky, naive, Headstrong, and at times, her own worst enemy. I found myself, one minute cheering her on, the next time, consoling her, and the next wanting to uncover the mysteries in her life for her, all the while shaking my head and laughing at her antics.

D. M. Bogacho has a way of making you feel like you know each of the characters in the book as well as feeling like you are part of their conversations.

BY AMY TRIPP-MAGUIRE.

PROLOGUE

Eight years earlier

My parents, along with my older brother, Frank, and my sister, Fiona and I, were on our way to the airport; Fiona and Frank were going to America to make their fortune. It was 1970. We were from a seaside town in England called Margate, Kent. It was famous for having beautiful beaches and excellent golf courses, which my father, John, managed. We were not wealthy but were comfortable. My grandparents, who were born and wed in America, came to England in the early 1900s. My grandfather was an out-of-work shipbuilder when he heard there were many jobs in Scotland and England. So, Grandpa Jim and Granny Alice headed to England for a better life. While living there, Grandpa Jim heard of a new ship being constructed in Ireland called the *Titanic*. The builders were looking for experienced riveters.

Together, they left Englands, Grampa's job and headed to Ireland because the wages they were offering were much better than in England. He was hired on the spot and worked as a riveter for a few years until the ship launched. As everyone knows, the *Titanic* sank on its maiden voyage to America in 1912. Every time I heard that story, I often thought: *What if my grandparents had wanted to go back to America on that ship? None of us would be here now.* After that tragedy, my grandfather and grandmother decided to move *back* to England to live—four years later, my mother was born.

Frank worked with my dad at the golf course as their accountant. He was twenty-four years old and frustrated with everything that was going on in England, which involved the unions, churches and schools. He had several former classmates who had ventured out to America and were doing very well. Besides, that is where our roots were, and he was determined to see it. It was a shock to my mum and dad when he announced several weeks back—he was leaving home. He felt there was nothing here for him. He secretly thought: *I do not want to spend my life at a golf course and be like my father.* My father was born in America but came here when he was twenty years old. Soon after, he met my mother.

Fiona immediately jumped on board when she heard what Frank's plans were to be, as this would also be her chance. She was twenty-three, worked as a paralegal in a small law firm, and wanted to explore other places. My mum was devastated that her two oldest children were leaving the nest. It wouldn't have been too bad, but *America*? The car ride to the airport was eerily quiet.

"When I get to be eighteen," I said, startling everyone, "I am going to America too!"

My mother looked at me and replied, "You are only ten years old; eighteen is a long way off, so don't talk nonsense. Your brother and sister will be back! You can bet on that."

But they didn't come back except to visit at Christmastime. Two years later, my sisters, Elsie and Alison, followed suit. The older I got, the more determined I was going to go too. A year after they left, my father took ill and passed away from heart failure. My mother was devastated. Fiona, Frank, Elsie and Alison came back for his funeral. They stayed about three weeks to help Mum get her finances in shape. As it turned out, my dad had left everything in excellent order—Mum would be okay financially. Pretty soon, we had to say goodbye to our four oldest siblings again. Although we understood why they had to get back to their jobs, we wished they could have stayed longer. Now there were just four kids, and my mom left at home. I was thirteen and entering the eighth grade; my brother, Daniel, was seventeen; Eileen just turned twenty-one, and Bonnie was nineteen and in college.

Eileen, Bonnie, and Daniel had no aspirations to leave England and their mother alone—for Mum had no desire to leave England. After all, her friends, relatives, and the remains of her husband were still here. On the other hand, I was still determined to leave when I was eighteen—and that is what I did the day after my eighteenth birthday.

Part ONE

"Carlos"

Chapter One

The year was 1978. I had just turned eighteen and was packing to fly to America. I can't tell you how excited I was about this adventure. I was accepted at Miami Dade College in Miami, Florida. It was close to where Fiona and Frank settled, and I had received an outstanding scholarship from the school. My mum gave me a large amount of my share of—what would have been—my inheritance when she died. I cried as I looked at the check.

"This should help you get established when you graduate and look for a place of your own," she said to me while holding back tears. "I know Fiona will let you stay with her for a while so that I won't worry." She then reached over and gave me the biggest hug I think I had ever received from her. I hugged her back.

I stared at my mother; she was starting to age. She was only sixty-one, but having eight children took their toll on her. Mum was forty-three when she had me. I was her *Miracle Child,* as she used to call me, and I was nervous about when I would see her again. I opened my presents from Daniel, Eileen and Bonnie. All and all, it was a great birthday send-off. I would be leaving in the morning for the airport; everyone would be coming to see me board the plane. It would be very hard for me to leave, but I knew this was something I had to do.

That night, I sat on my bed and studied everything in my room; I didn't want to forget anything. I had already taken pictures of each room in the house, also the outside yard. I just went around and snapped pictures. I wanted to remember *everything.* I must have taken a hundred photos of my mother, sisters and brother. As I looked at my photo album, I picked out a particular picture of my mum and dad holding me as a baby. I was taking this photo with me. I smiled as I got into my bed. *Would I be able to fall asleep?* I was so excited. This would be my first time flying, and the fact that I was going all by myself gave me a real sense of pride. Soon sleep came—then my alarm screamed in my ear.

When I heard it, I flew out of bed and headed to my bathroom. I had one hour before we were to leave for the airport. *Was this really happening to me? America, here I come.*

"MacKenzie, are you up?" my mother yelled to me from the bottom of the stairs.

I yelled down to her that I was, and I was going to take a shower. "Be right down," I added. I wasn't sure she heard me, but she didn't answer me back — it must mean she did.

Within fifteen minutes, I was showered and dressed. I grabbed my suitcases and headed downstairs. I had about a half-hour to eat, and then we would be headed to the airport. To my surprise, my mother had made a massive breakfast for us—everything *I* liked! We all sat down and dug in. We chatted and reminisced about everything. We all missed our father and wished he were here with us, especially me. Dad and I had a special bond, probably because I was his youngest child. As a toddler, I followed him everywhere I could. I grinned, thinking of him. I loved and missed him so much, and I knew he would be proud of me.

Finally, it was time to head to the airport. My mother told me my airplane was a new plane which carried four hundred people. It was going to fly to J.F.K. Airport in New York City. I would change planes and then fly to Miami International Airport. It would be a long, exhausting trip. I brought my magazines and a book to read—I was all set. My total flight time till I reached Miami would be about ten hours. Ugh!

My goodbyes to my sisters and brother were very emotional. The hardest, though, was saying goodbye to my mother. She had always been there for me, and now I will be practically on my own—making my own decisions. Of course, I would still have Fiona and Frank close by to talk about things—I was glad of that. Elsie and Alison settled up in the New England area when they went to America. I had hoped that once I was settled and on my school break, I would be able to travel up north to see them. Let my adventure begin!

"MacKenzie, do you have everything? Your passport, student visa card?" She was anxious when we arrived at the airport.

"Yes, yes, Mum. I have everything I need. Don't worry." I gave everyone their last hug and kiss. As I turned to leave them behind, I gave them a big smile and waved confidently. "Bye," I said one last time. I thought I saw my mum's head fall to her chest. I knew she was crying, but she would be okay. She and my dad had raised powerful independent children.

I checked my luggage and then went to the line to show my passport and other papers I had brought. The gentleman who stamped and looked through everything barely looked at me, as he was just pushing people along. I wondered what it was going to be like when I reached America and got off the plane. I assumed I would have to go through the same things again—but I didn't; it was much more manageable. I looked at my tickets and then went to the terminal listed on them. There were so many people waiting to board. I no sooner sat down when they called the first set of passengers. Many people stood up, so I did too; I wasn't sure when I would be called. My number was seventy-five. I found out I would be in the next group of people. After several minutes, they announced passengers seventy-five through one hundred and fifty would be next. *Well, here I go.* My stomach was doing some flips; I just followed the crowd, though. I found my seat quickly and was happy I was by the window. I put my carry-on up above and sat down next to two empty seats. I had hoped I would be by myself, but it wasn't to be. Within a few minutes, an older gentleman sat in the middle, and his wife, I assumed, sat on the aisle seat. They looked at me and smiled—I smiled back.

My mother told me not to talk to too many strangers; be polite, but distant. I quickly got my book out and started to read, and waited for the boarding to end. The stewardess finally got up and proceeded to teach us all what to do in an emergency, where the bathrooms were, and that snacks would be coming around in a little bit. *Then it happened!* The plane began to back up slowly. I watched out the window as it left the airport terminal and proceeded to the runway to await instructions for take-off. *Will this vast aircraft be able to lift off the ground?*

I strapped myself in as the plane headed down the runway, faster and faster it went. My head was forced back against the seat. *Up, up* we went. I suddenly felt very nervous. *When will it level off?* I squeezed my eyes shut, holding onto my seat. Finally, it started to straighten out when the captain came on the intercom to introduce himself and welcomed us all aboard. He told us the weather would be great for traveling and that New York City was sunny. I let out a big sigh of relief. When I opened my eyes, my neighbors were staring at me and smiling.

"First time flying?" they asked in unison.

"Yes, I am on my way to attend college in Florida. I have sisters and a brother living in the states." I smiled. *Why did I tell them all that? Sorry, Mum.*

"We fly all the time, so don't worry." the man said while patting my hand. "My name is Jeff, and this is my wife, June," he added.

I smiled at them and told them my name. I began to read, and after a while, I was feeling sleepy. I closed my book and took a quick peek out the window, but I couldn't see much because of the clouds. I laid my head back against the seat and soon fell asleep. The next thing I knew, the stewardess asked what I wanted for lunch; there were two choices. I picked the chicken sandwich and a soda. She thanked me and moved on down the row.

We were soon served our lunches, and then clean-up began. I was amazed at how efficient they seemed. I looked at my watch and realized I had been asleep for three hours. I knew when we landed that I had to turn my clock back five hours. It was so confusing to me. England was five hours ahead of New York. I decided I would fix my watch to the correct time now so I wouldn't forget when we landed. It was four o'clock in England but eleven o'clock a.m. in New York. We had four more hours of flying time, so I picked up my book and began reading again.

After a while, I put it down as I was getting bored. I wanted to use the restroom but was afraid to disturb Jeff and June. I think they sensed that I needed to get up for a bit because Jeff asked me if I needed to use the restroom. *Was it that obvious?* I said yes, and that I felt bad they had to stand up to let me out of my seat. He just grinned at me and told me it was not a problem. When I sat back down, Jeff, June, and I started to chat a little. It helped me pass the time. Before we knew it, the stewardess was coming around with more drinks and snacks to hand out. I thought that was cool. We had about two more hours of flying time before we would be landing. I was very excited; I couldn't wait to see Fiona and Frank, as they would be waiting for me.

After about an hour, the captain came on the intercom again and told us he would begin the descent. The plane would feel a little weird as it dropped altitude, he told us. Nothing to worry about, he added; it was all a natural occurrence. I thought it felt funny, but okay. It was pretty subtle, so I picked up my crossword puzzle magazine and started to play. Jeff was a big help to me because I was stumped many times—he was a brilliant man.

Every so often, I peeked out the window, and I could tell things were changing. There were no more clouds, just a pretty blue sky, and before long, we started to decelerate every once in a while. I heard the engines grind. Then the wheels came down, and that meant we were so close to landing. Soon I could see little tiny buildings, and as we got closer, they became recognizable. The captain once again came on and told us to buckle our seatbelts because we would be landing in about twenty minutes. I felt the tears in my eyes. I did this all by myself—I was so proud.

Chapter Two

I felt the wheels touch down on the runway. I had made it to New York, but I still had to disembark, go to a smaller plane, and then head to Florida. Hopefully, I wouldn't get lost because this airport was so much bigger than the one in England. As I got off the plane, Jeff and June came up to wish me a safe trip down south.

"It has been a pleasure to know you, young lady." He extended his hand. I was surprised when June came over to me and hugged me. I had told them I would be fine, and it was a pleasure meeting them also. During our chat on the plane, I found out they were going home to New York after spending ten days vacationing in England. They were friendly people. I don't know why my mother was so worried.

I was glad that all the luggage I had checked in would be transferred to the next plane for me. I thought that was great. All I had to lug around was my pocketbook and my carry-on, which was on wheels. Perfect! I guess I must have looked confused because a woman approached me and asked if I needed any help finding my terminal. I knew she worked there because I saw a badge hanging around her neck. I replied that I was a little lost, and I showed her my ticket. She told me to follow her, and it wasn't far, so I did.

I didn't think Mum would approve of my socializing, but what else could I do? I was much more trusting than she was. In a few minutes, we arrived at the correct terminal. I thanked the lady for her help, and she said to have a safe trip to Florida. Everyone was so kind to me. The airport was very crowded, and I thought it would be a smaller plane, but there seemed to be too many people. I mentioned it to someone who was standing like I was. He just laughed and remarked that there was another plane at the other door, and all the seating was combined, so it looked like everyone was together. I thought that was a dumb setup. It was too confusing to me.

Pretty soon, it was time to board. At least this time I didn't feel so lost because I knew the procedure. When I found my seat, I realized there were only two seats together instead of three. It was a smaller plane. It would take us between three and three and a half hours to get to Miami—I couldn't wait.

I dozed most of the way. The flight was smooth, but I noticed they only offered a small snack and a drink about an hour into the flight. I knew I was starving because my stomach kept making noises; I was embarrassed. The lady next to me didn't seem to notice, though. I wished I had had the time to grab something to eat at the terminal in New York. I suddenly became brave and asked the stewardess if I could have cookies *and* chips, as I was famished. She smiled and gave me both. *Gee, everyone is so lovely to me.*

I soon felt that same sensation as the larger plane when it descended to a lower altitude but on a smaller scale. Then, I felt the wheels come down, and before I knew it—we landed. *Miami, Florida, are you ready for MacKenzie Ables?* I couldn't get off the plane quick enough. I grabbed my carry-on and pocketbook, and I proceeded to walk through the door. It only took me a few seconds to find them. They were jumping up and down, waving to me as I left the waiting area. I finally made it—it was a very long trip.

"MacKenzie," my sister shouted while running to me. She gave me a huge hug and asked if my flight was okay. I told her that both trips were flawless, and I loved them. Frank came over to me, picked me up, and twirled me around.

"I am so relieved to see you. A person's first time is always a little traumatic. You did okay?" he was smiling. He had a great smile and perfectly straight teeth. He reminded me of Dad.

"Wow, you guys look wonderful. You are both so tan." I said to them.

"Wait till you feel the heat. It is May, and the temperature is in the 80's. We go to the beach all year practically." Fiona said to me. "You will love it here."

"Okay, let's go get your luggage and get the heck out of here," Frank said as he grabbed my carry-on and proceeded to head to the baggage area. Fiona and I followed. *Thank God for big brothers.*

On the ride to Fiona's house, she was busy pointing out all the sights. To me, it was as if I was in a different world. I knew about palm trees and had seen pictures, of course, but to see them in person is unbelievable! Fiona was right when she said it was hot out. The weather in England in May is around 11-16 Celsius, which is about 60 degrees. It was a real treat. I thought it funny that Americans drove on the wrong side of the street. So many differences I would have to get used to surviving. Technically, I was a citizen of England, but since my parents were American, I am American even though I was born in England. However, there would be paperwork to file, so I would have proof if I needed it. It wasn't very easy for me when my mother explained everything, but I think I have all the up-to-date documents I will need. I have a valid driver's license from England; I should be okay driving in America with that license. *So many things to consider.*

Before long, we arrived at the condo Fiona had purchased a year ago in Coral Gables. From the outside, it looked beautiful; I was very excited to see the inside of where I would be staying.

"Well, Mac," as Fiona called me, "here we are. My place is the last one on the right."

We unloaded the car and carried my luggage into the condo. It was a single unit attached to two other units. It looked like a bunch of tiny homes attached. She had two floors: three bedrooms upstairs with two full baths, and a kitchen combo dining room, one-half bath in the laundry room, and a large living room downstairs. It was something I had never seen before.

Although I had slept on the plane rides, I was still exhausted because of the time change. Fiona suggested I take a short nap while she cooked dinner; she added she had something to tell me when I was rested. Frank said he had to go back to his place and he would see me tomorrow. We hugged, and I thanked him. I agreed that I was exhausted.

Fiona helped me bring my bags upstairs and showed me my bedroom and bathroom. I couldn't believe it. Everything was so beautiful. My room was a blue color with white woodwork and white curtains. A few pictures hung here and there on the walls, also a lovely queen-sized bed, a dresser, and a comfy chair—not too crowded. When I looked into the closet, I gasped because I could walk right in it—it was huge. *I am going to like living here!*

Chapter Three

After sleeping for about an hour, I felt Fiona shaking me and saying dinner was almost ready. I looked up at her groggily and asked her if I had time to take a shower, as I felt sweaty from traveling so long on the plane.

"Absolutely, then come down for dinner," she said, touching the tip of my nose just like Mum did.

It didn't take me too long. I showered, washed my hair, and changed into my nightclothes. I was ready for bed. I looked at the clock, and it was six-thirty, which meant it was eleven-thirty in England. Mum would be getting ready for bed. I decided to call her to let her know I had arrived safely. When I talked to her, she started to cry, and then mentioned that Frank had called her when my plane landed. We talked for a few minutes, and then I said I would call tomorrow and chat longer with her. I was glad there was a phone in my room to use anytime I wished.

We had a nice dinner of shrimp and pasta; I was famished. After we ate, I helped her clear the dishes and put them into the dishwasher. We then went into the living room and sat down. I was anxious to hear what she was going to discuss with me.

Fiona told me that she was married. I was shocked because she hadn't informed our mother or our siblings in England. I asked when this was, and she said it was one year ago. She told me it was a small wedding, and she did not invite anyone but Frank. I didn't understand what the big deal was.

"That is not all; you have two beautiful nieces. My husband, Don, had two small children by his ex-wife and received custody of the children. I met Don two years ago, and we fell in love. Then last year, we decided to become a family. You see, Mac, I can't have any children. I discovered it when I first came here and had a terrible infection, which left me without viable working ovaries. I almost died. I didn't want to tell anyone because I was devastated. When I met Don, he was a male nurse at the hospital. He was wonderful to me, and there was an instant attraction. After I got well, we started to date, and the rest is history. Mum would never have understood. I didn't want to worry anyone. I am so sorry." She sighed with great relief.

At first, I couldn't think of anything to say, then I got up and went over to her, gave her a big hug, and told her I was sorry for what she went through but was *so* happy for her. I couldn't wait to meet her family. "When will I get to meet them?" I asked her.

"Tomorrow after work. I have to go into my office for a while, and then I will have the rest of the week to spend with you. I don't live here at the condo. I live with Don at his house across town. We usually rent the condo out, as it was bought as an investment for Don and me. You will stay here because our house is small and there isn't an extra bedroom. Will you be okay with that? You could walk to our house from here. It is only a couple of miles away," she said with a grin on her face. I told her I would love to stay here and asked what the rent would be because I had my money from Mum. Nothing right now, she told me, as it would only be for four months because I would be in a college dorm in August. I felt so grown up and mature—I was going to live on my own for the first time in my life.

Fiona said she would stay here for a couple of nights till I felt comfortable with everything. We talked for a few more hours. She told me Frank had a girlfriend, and he owned his own used-car lot. It was all high-end vehicles: Cadillacs, Lincolns, BMWs, and other expensive cars. I told her I had heard that from our mother. *Apparently, not everything was kept from Mum!* After a while, I began to yawn a lot. Fiona chuckled and told me to get to bed; we would talk more tomorrow after work, and she probably would be gone before I woke up but would be home by noon. I hugged and kissed her; I told her I loved her as I walked up the stairs to bed.

The morning came very quickly to me. It seemed I had just laid down in the dark, and now the bright sunshine was beaming through the windows. I stretched and yawned a couple of times and made myself get up out of bed. I needed to unpack my suitcases and hang up my clothes in my *giant* closet! After putting things away, I decided to get dressed and go downstairs to eat breakfast. As I entered the kitchen, I noticed Fiona had put out a cereal bowl and silverware, my favorite box of cereal, and a coffee cup set up by the coffeemaker with fresh coffee brewing. I opened the refrigerator, and it was stocked with many things. I grabbed milk and juice and sat down at the island, eating like there was no tomorrow. There were even fresh donuts on a plate with plastic wrap over them. She had thought of everything. While eating, I called my mother, and we talked for about an hour. I never mentioned Fiona being married, though. I thought that information should come from her. I will speak to her this afternoon about confiding in our mum. I felt my mother would be happy for her.

After I ate, I decided to go outside and take a walk and look around the area. As I walked towards the door, I noticed a set of keys on the counter. *She thinks of everything.* Fiona must have known I would want to take a little tour of the place outside. Her leaving the keys was a hint for me to lock the door behind me. I chuckled to myself—nope, this isn't England—we hardly ever locked our doors

I thought I was in *paradise.* The air was balmy and very warm, hot actually. There were the beautiful palm trees I saw spread up and down the street when I arrived last night. I walked around the back of the complex and noticed there were two in-ground pools. One was rectangular, and the other one was shaped like a kidney. *I am the luckiest person in the world right now!* I decided to explore down the street because I wanted to walk every day somewhere and get to know the area. I should be okay if I stay on the sidewalks.

I walked down one street, then up another, and then around a corner, just walking and thinking. My mistake was that I was not noticing street signs, and a couple of times, I had crossed over to another area. *What was I thinking?* I kept walking and changing directions. It then dawned on me that I was lost! Everything looked the same—condo after condo. What was the name of Fiona's condo? I couldn't even remember the color. Was it a light pink? Blue? Maybe white? Did I pass that food mart before? *What an idiot I am.* I looked at my watch and realized I had to be back at the condo soon. "I had to have been walking for about an hour," I thought to myself.

I looked over at the store and saw a young man with one leg bent back with his foot leaning on a palm tree; he was trying to light a cigarette and was having trouble because the breeze kept blowing out his match. He then saw me and put the cigarette away, and started to walk over towards me. He had tan skin and a mustache. On his head, he was wearing a handkerchief backward. "What should I do? Should I run?" I thought. He was coming closer to me with a smile on his face. He looked friendly; maybe he could help me. I stayed put.

"Hi there," he said to me. "You look confused. Are you lost?"

"I think I am, a little. I am staying in my sister's condo, but I kind of wandered a little too far. I'm from England and am going to register for the fall at the college this afternoon." *Why did I say all that?* "This is my first trip to America" His eyes were mesmerizing, a deep chocolate brown color. Then I added, "Do you think you could help me?"

"I will certainly try. I will be a senior at the college this fall. By the way, my name is Carlito Perez—Carlos for short."

My heart did a flip. "Oh, thank you so much. My name is MacKenzie Ables. I am afraid I don't remember much; I feel so stupid that I didn't check the name of the street."

"No problem, we will figure it out. There are only about four different complexes within a two-mile radius. Try and remember something about the place you are staying in," he said confidently. He then added, "It isn't the one across the street, so that leaves three left."

I thought and thought, and then I remembered there was a McDonald's across the street. When I told him that, he knew exactly where it was. He told me it was called the "The Green Gables." He said it was called that because all the condos were a pastel green color.

A picture flashed in my head; yes, the buildings *were* green. "Oh, thank you so much for your help. Which way is it?"

He grabbed my hand and told me to come with him; he knew a shortcut. I don't know why I trusted him, but I let him lead the way. In about a half-hour, we were there. When I saw Fiona's car, I was relieved. He held my hand for a few seconds before letting go and mentioned that, maybe, he would see me again at the college this afternoon. He had some papers to sign that had to do with working on campus. I thanked him again and told him I would be there in a few hours. When he smiled at me, all I could think was that his teeth were the whitest I had ever seen. He waved to me as he left the complex area, and I waved back. At that moment, Fiona came out the door frantically.

"Where were you? Who was that?" She was anxious. "You scared me when you were not home when I got here. Where did you go?"

"Calm down, Fiona. I just wandered a little, and I might have lost my way, as everything looks the same here. Carlos helped me find my way back, no harm done!" I didn't tell her that we would probably bump into him when we went to the college after lunch. What was the point!

Chapter Four

After we ate lunch; we headed over to the college so I could register for the fall. I gathered all the necessary papers together, and soon we were on our way. On the way over, I didn't talk much because I was thinking of Carlos. His name sounded Mexican or Cuban; I wasn't sure. I kept visualizing his smile and his white teeth. He was adorable, and I was secretly hoping I would run into him. Fiona interrupted my thoughts.

"Why are you so quiet?" she asked. "Are you nervous about the interview today? Don't be because I know you will do very well. You have what it takes to become a lawyer if that is really what you want to be."

"I am quiet because I am just taking in the sights. It is so different than England. Yes, I do want to become a lawyer, and I know it won't be easy, Fiona. Dad always told me I could be anything I wanted as long as I did the work."

"That sounds like Dad. Can I just make one suggestion to you?" she looked at me, and when I nodded, she continued, "I think you should take courses to become a paralegal and use it as a secondary major. It would only take about six months to receive your degree in that field. That way, if, for some reason, you change your mind about becoming a lawyer, you will have something to fall back on. I also think it would come in handy because you could work alongside licensed lawyers. It would be great training, and you could work part-time while finishing up your degree," she paused and then said, "What do you think?"

She was brilliant. I wondered why she never went on to become a lawyer. "You know, Fiona, I think that would be a good idea. I will consider it." I could tell my sister was very pleased with herself. I knew she was happy I hadn't rejected the idea.

"And one more thing," Fiona added, "you could probably work for the same group of lawyers I work for. They hire college students for part-time work. I know I could get you in." The next thing I knew, she was pulling into the parking lot in front of the administration offices.

I looked at her and put my hands to my mouth as if I was biting my nails. She laughed at me. "This is something you have to do on your own, I'm afraid. I will be waiting out here in the car for you. Go get 'em!" I opened the door, grabbed my folders, and blew her a kiss as I left the car.

When my interview was over, I was very pleased with myself. After I left the office and started walking down the hall, I looked around, hoping to see Carlos. I was disappointed I had missed him. Just as I was about to open the door and leave the building, he entered.

"Hey, hi there, I was hoping I would run into you here. How did it go, MacKenzie?" he said to me.

H*e remembered my name*! "Carlos? How are you?" I thought that was stupid to say. "I am pretty sure I did okay. They were very helpful in helping me pick my courses." My heart was beating very rapidly. He then asked if we could go for coffee sometime—I could have died. "Ah, ah," I became tongue-tied for a few seconds. "That sounds like fun. I could meet you somewhere, maybe tomorrow. I don't have a car, though, so I would have to walk. If you could direct me, maybe I could find it."

He laughed a little. "How about I meet you across the street at McDonald's—say around ten?" I told him that would be perfect and then went out the door.

Fiona was waiting outside the car, smoking a cigarette. When she saw me, she threw it on the ground and stepped on it; I had no idea she smoked and pretended I didn't see it. I went running down the steps and jumped into the car, and let out a little scream. I was so excited.

"I did it! I did it!" I shouted at her. "Everything went perfectly. They were accommodating. Yes, I am going to take classes to become a paralegal. I am doing nights this summer. By the time I start college, I will be a paralegal. Great idea, sis." I reached over and gave her a peck on the cheek.

"I am so happy for you, Mac. It is going to be a great summer. Now I will take you over to meet my family, and then we can swing by Frank's place if you like."

This day was turning out to be one of my most incredible days. I felt a little guilty not mentioning that I ran into Carlos. I didn't want or need a lecture from her or anyone. I certainly would not tell her of my meeting with him tomorrow—it is only coffee, for crying out loud!

After about a half-hour, we turned into a small development of smaller homes. It was on the outskirts of Coral Gables. All the lawns were well-manicured. The streets were lined with red maples. As we turned into her lane, I noticed many young kids playing in the street and their yards. I knew this was perfect for Fiona, something she had always wanted. I was excited to meet Fiona's husband and stepchildren. As soon as the car pulled into the driveway, two little kids, about six or seven years old, came running up to the vehicle.

"FiFi. FiFi," they yelled at her.

Fiona jumped out of the car and scooped both little girls up in her arms. Hi babies, I want you to meet my sister, MacKenzie. You may call her Auntie Mac if you like."

"Hi there," I said to them. "What are your names?" I asked. They shyly stayed behind Fiona.

"The blond one is Maria, she's six, and the brunette is Margo; she is seven." It was Don's voice as he came out of the house.

He came right over to me and hugged me. "You look just like Fiona, except a little shorter. Welcome to America!"

"Thank you, Don. So far, so good. I just registered for college, and I am really excited about being here. Your little girls are so adorable."

"Well, come in, and Fiona and the girls will show you around while I get back to my barbecue. I hope you like burgers and potato salad."

I told him I did, and after we looked inside the house, we went out back and had a nice dinner on their patio. I was very envious of Fiona. I knew someday this was what I would like for myself—not right away, though!

After dinner, we went to see Frank. The whole day, except my getting lost, was terrific. I felt very comfortable and thrilled to be here in America.

Chapter Five

Fiona was to stay one more night then was going home because she missed everyone. Tomorrow, when she got home from work, she would show me everything she thought I should know about this condo. Also, we were going to take a little driving trip with me at the wheel.

"I will try and get out earlier tomorrow; I should be home by two. Please don't go far; I don't want you getting lost again." She smiled at me.

We stayed up talking for a while, and she showed me where the circuit breakers were and what breaker did what, just in case I tripped one of them. We discussed places she wanted to show me in the coming weeks. I said I was very excited about being here and not to worry about me.

"Mac, is there one place that you really want to go or have heard about?" she asked.

Without much hesitation, I looked at her and practically yelled the words. "*Disney World.*" She laughed and told me she knew that was coming out of my mouth at some point.

"We will definitely get there. I went the first year I came here, and it was a truly wonderful experience. However, it's about four hours away. It will have to be an overnight adventure—maybe two. I want to wait till late fall or Christmastime when it isn't as hot, and I want to take Maria and Margo the next time I go; they have never been."

I agreed with her. "I would love to go and see Maria and Margo experience this for the first time along with me." Around ten o'clock, we decided to call it a night.

When I woke up, Fiona had already left for work. I was so excited to meet Carlos at McDonald's. I jumped out of bed and took a shower. I went to my *huge* walk-in closet—I will never get used to the size of it—and looked for something to wear. Everything I looked at, I hated. I thought to myself that I must go shopping for some new clothes as soon as I learn how to drive on the opposite side of the street! I was very nervous about practicing this afternoon. I finally found something that looked like I had always lived in America. They dressed a little differently than we did in England, and I wanted to fit in.

It was 8:30, and I had plenty of time. I decided to have a bowl of cereal to eat because Carlos just mentioned coffee—not breakfast! After I had finished, I cleared and did the dishes and put them away. I then ran upstairs to do my hair and makeup. As I looked in the mirror, I made a face. I really needed a haircut. I will add that to things I had to do; I was keeping a list.

It was now 9:45. I flew out the door and went to the street to cross over. The traffic was hefty. I went to the crosswalk and pressed the button; cars halted to let me cross within seconds. I made sure I waved thank you to them even though they were required by law to stop and let me cross. In England, we do have busy streets, but they were mainly in the big cities. There are a little over 6,000 people living in my community. I read somewhere that the population in Miami was well over 340,000 people! I hurried over to McDonald's and looked for Carlos. It was precisely 10 o'clock; I was right on time. I didn't see him anywhere outside, so I went inside and looked around—he wasn't there. When I went out again, I saw him. He was sitting in his car smoking with his hand held outside of the window. I don't think he noticed me walking towards the car.

"Carlos?" I said almost in a whisper. He turned and looked at me and smiled as he flicked his cigarette to the ground. It remained lit, so I quickly went over and stepped on it. "I didn't want some child to pick it up and try it," I said, embarrassed.

"No, of course not. Sorry about that. Get in." he ordered. I was hesitant; I really didn't know him at all. "I just want to talk a bit; I promise I won't kidnap you, honest." He snickered as his eyes penetrated my core. I knew I shouldn't.

He reached over and unlocked the passenger door. I went around to the passenger side and hopped in without shutting the door entirely in case I had to run. "Are we going to get coffee here?" I asked him.

"We can if you would like to, but I wanted to take you to a great coffee shop a couple of streets over that's maybe five minutes away. Is that okay?"

My heart was pounding so hard; I thought he probably could hear it. I was afraid I would seem like a baby if I said no. "Yes, that's okay," I replied. "I want to find different places around that I can walk to if I feel like it." All the while, I had my fingers crossed that he was on the up and up. *This was so unlike me!*

"I have one question for you," he paused. "How come you don't have an accent?" he glanced at me as he drove.

It was my time to smile at him. "Well, the short version is: My Mum and Dad are American. My grandparents came over to England in 1910 from America. My mother was born there, and my dad came over when he was twenty-something. He met my mother, and the rest is history. Just like my parents, I actually have dual citizenship also."

"Wow, interesting. My parents are from Cuba, and they still live there. I came over here to go to school with my brother when I was about seventeen. We stayed with an uncle. I never went back. Someday soon, I *will* go back, though." He turned into a small plaza. I noticed a little coffee shop. I think I passed it when I had gotten lost.

We went inside, and it was pretty nice. It was decorated with items from the fifties and sixties. I felt like I traveled into a time warp. "Very nice," I replied. "I have never been in a place quite like this before. Thank you for bringing me here."

"You're welcome; I'm glad you like it. I come here a lot. I love to play the jukebox. Are there any requests?" I told him anything he wanted to play was okay by me. He walked over to the machine and put a few quarters in. An Elvis song played first. We sat near the jukebox, and he asked if I had eaten breakfast. I said that I had because he never mentioned breakfast before, only coffee.

"I haven't eaten yet," he explained, "do you mind if I order something for myself? Why don't you have a muffin or something with your coffee?" he suggested.

"That's a great idea. I will, thank you." We chit-chatted for about an hour. He described his life in Cuba, and I told him about my family and things I did in England. It was a really great time, and I thought he was very nice. When it was time to take me home, he asked if he could see me again. I had told him I didn't see why not. We made plans to go out on Saturday night. Now I *definitely* needed to do a little shopping—another perfect day under my belt. I was happy!

When we got back to Green Gables, I was tempted to ask if he wanted to come in—but I didn't. I still had a few hours before Fiona got back, but if she ever came home early, well, she would hit the roof. As I started to get out of the car, I felt his hand on my arm; I turned towards him, and he leaned in and kissed me ever so gently on my lips. That was only the second time I had been kissed by anyone who *wasn't* my relative. I put my fingers to my lips and rubbed them. "I will see you Saturday at seven. You can pick me up here." I smiled and then ran up the few stairs and unlocked the door. I turned and gave a wave as I went inside.

I sat on the couch and watched some television, and waited for Fiona to come home. I wrestled with the notion that I should tell her I went for coffee with Carlos. What could she say? Even if she disapproved of this whole thing, I was eighteen and on my own—still, I didn't want to get on her wrong side. I decided I would tell her on Saturday that I had a date with him. I glanced at the phone that was in the living area. *I should probably call Mum.* I prepared a snack, then picked up the phone and dialed my mother's number.

Chapter Six

When Fiona came back, she sat in the car and honked the horn a couple of times. I had just hung up the phone after having a pleasant conversation with my mother. I went to the door and opened it; she yelled for me to come on and that I was going to drive. I waved at her and went to grab my pocketbook. I quickly looked inside to make sure I had my license with me.

"What took you so long, Mac? It will be easy." She was now sitting on the passenger side, which was the wrong side as far as I was concerned.

"Don't you think it's a little too soon?" I asked her, "I'm really nervous about this."

As I proceeded to back slowly out of the driveway onto the street, she told me it wouldn't take long before I was used to it. She took me down many side streets for a while, then directed me to the main road. It was bustling as people were coming home from work. We drove around for about an hour. I was surprised at myself—how fast I caught on. The scariest part was a right or left turn; I felt it was very awkward for me. She showed me the nearest mall to the condo, and I also drove to the college where I would be taking my night classes. I kiddingly said that these were the only two places I would go to, so she needn't worry.

"Tomorrow I will take you to Frank's dealership. He told me he had found the perfect car for you to drive." She smiled at me.

"Can I take your car tomorrow after we check out my car? I want to drive to the mall by myself and do a little shopping for some new things to wear. I really need to fill that *huge* closet!" I laughed a little.

"That's okay by me. We will go to my house, and you can head out from there. Margo and Maria have been asking for you anyway. Why don't you stay for dinner? By the time you come back, I will have something ready for all of us. Sound like a plan?"

I told her it sounded great. After my driving lesson, she brought me back to the condo then drove off—I was relieved. I loved my sister, but I loved my time alone too. That night I went through my clothes and planned a shopping strategy. Tomorrow was Friday, and it was going to be a busy day. I wasn't sure when I would tell Fiona about my date on Saturday. Maybe I wouldn't mention it at all.

I fixed myself a sandwich and then went into the living room to watch some TV. After a short while, I found myself drifting off to sleep; I thought maybe I was still on England time. I couldn't quite make it through the whole evening, but I would be up too early if I slept now. Fiona said that it took her at least a week to start feeling at home and getting used to the time difference. She was right! So much had happened to me in just a couple of days. I decided I would go upstairs, take a shower, and then get to bed. I was excited about purchasing my vehicle even though it wouldn't be new. If I know Frank, this car will be a special one for me. When I was in bed, I kept thinking of Carlos and our up-and-coming date on Saturday. I couldn't get his pearly whites and his little mustache above his lip out of my head. I put my fingers on my lips, remembering his kiss. Soon I felt myself drifting off.

Brr-ring, brr-ring! The sound of the bedroom phone woke me up with a start. I reached over and picked it up and sleepily said hello to the caller. It was Fiona.

"Mac, did I wake you?" she asked with excitement in her voice.

It took me a second, and I said to her with a yawn and a stretch, "Yeah, you did. What time do you get up anyway?" I asked her while wiping the sleep from my eyes so I could look at the alarm clock. It read eight a.m.; I groaned.

"Oh, I'm so sorry, Mac. I didn't mean to wake you up. I have been thinking about today and am so excited. I took the day off. What time did you want to go to Frank's place?" she asked me and then added, "Aren't you excited about getting your own car?"

"Yes, of course, I am. I didn't think it would be this early, though. Please give me a couple of hours, Okay? You forget I am not a morning person." I smiled to myself. *What if I didn't like the car that he picked out?*

"Okay, how about ten or so?"

I told her that would be fine and then hung up and laid back down. I didn't want to get up till nine. I closed my eyes for a few minutes trying to motivate myself to get up and get dressed. After a short while, I got up and went to my closet to find something to wear. By then, my stomach had started to tell me it was hungry. I went downstairs and made my breakfast; then I went back up to finish my hair and makeup. *I must get a haircut soon.* I had just gotten downstairs when I heard a car pull up in my driveway.

I opened the door and gave a wave to Fiona. "I'll just be a minute," I yelled to her.

When I went outside, she was in the passenger seat again. I went up to the window, and she pointed to the driver's seat. I was hoping I would be able to relax a little, but I guess I should be practicing as much as I can.

"If you want to take my car this afternoon, you need to practice more," she lectured.

"Yes, you're right," I said as I got into the car. "Let's go get my car!"

It was a little easier today driving on the wrong side of the street. "Why can't all countries do it the same way?" I wondered to myself. In about a half-hour, we pulled into Frank's used-car lot. "It was pretty fancy for a used car place," I thought. As I looked around, none of the vehicles *looked* old! I commented to Fiona and she said it was because all the cars were high-end used cars. The people who owned them had been well off financially. I was hoping I would be able to afford one of these *high-end* vehicles.

Frank immediately came out the door with a big grin on his face. "Hey there, beautiful, are you excited? I picked out three different makes and models," he smiled at me. I could tell he was very proud of himself. At least I would have a choice between three.

After much contemplation, I finally picked the smaller of the three. It was an older BMW. It was black and in excellent condition. It was twelve years old. When I sat in the driver's seat, I felt so mature and like a genuine adult. Frank said I could have it by Monday. I was so happy. I put down half of the money, and he would set up the financing for the rest through the bank they always used for their customers. He had given me the car for the price they purchased it for. I was so blessed. I thanked him and hugged him, and said I would see him on Monday. We headed over to Fiona's place, and then I would be on my own for a couple of hours. I couldn't wait.

Fiona had written the directions to the mall from her house. It would be an adventure driving with no co-pilot—I knew I could do it, however.

I found the mall with no problem. When I parked the car, I made sure I had picked a spot where there were not many cars around me. God forbid someone accidentally hits the car with a door or something. I didn't need anything to knock me off of the high I was feeling.

After a few hours, I was finished shopping. I bought several outfits that I absolutely loved on me. It was now time to drive back over to Fiona's house for dinner. I couldn't wait to see the girls and Don again. I hoped I would be able to find my way back.

As it turned out, my evening with my new family was beautiful. We laughed and told stories. I actually sat with the girls, and we built things with clay and then moved on to Legos. Soon it was time for me to go. Margo begged me to stay the night; she was so adorable. I had to explain to her that I couldn't because I wanted to go home and relax and call my mother, who lived very far away, but I would see them on Sunday morning. Fiona had suggested we all go out to breakfast—their treat.

When Don dropped me off, I realized I didn't mention to anyone about my date with Carlos. I knew, in my heart, they wouldn't understand, so it was just as well. I will tell Fiona on Sunday at breakfast. I was tired by the time I entered the house. It had been a busy day, and all I wanted to do was get undressed and call my mother. I did miss her very much.

Chapter Seven

On Saturday morning, I decided I would try to find a place to have my hair cut. I was pretty sure I had spotted a salon when I had gotten lost taking my walk a few days ago. I decided to venture out, again, to look. Sure enough, I spotted one and walked right in—it was not crowded, and they took me right away.

I was delighted with the results. I then decided to find the little cafe Carlos had taken me to when we had breakfast. After going down a couple of small streets, I saw it. I wondered if he would be in there. *Should I go in and see?* I was hungry, and I thought I would just buy a muffin and a coffee, but if he were there—I wouldn't go in. As I opened the door, I ran right into him while he was leaving with some friends.

"MacKenzie?" he said with a look of surprise on his face. "What are you doing here? You're not *lost* again, are you?" he smirked.

I stuttered a little, and he caught me by surprise. "No, I'm not *lost*! I just had my hair done a few streets over and thought I would come here for coffee and a muffin." I was embarrassed.

"Your hair looks nice. Well, I have to head out and can't talk now. I will catch you later." he turned and quickly said something to one of his friends, and then they left.

Well, that wasn't nice. He didn't even introduce me to his friends and never mentioned tonight. "What does that all mean?" I thought. I had hoped we were still going out. I realized I did not have a phone number for him, nor did he have mine. I guess I will have to wait and see, and I was glad I hadn't mentioned us going out to anyone, as it might not happen. I will be ready just in case. I really liked him a lot, and I thought he wanted me also. I didn't feel much like eating at the cafe, so I ordered everything to go—I was only a short way from the condo. When I arrived home, the phone was ringing. I quickly ran over to pick it up; it was Fiona.

"Hey, hi. I was just wondering if you wanted to come over tonight for a while."

"I'm going to pass for tonight," I said. I just got back from having my hair cut, and I wanted to go through my stuff and sort things out. I just want to chill. I threw something together when I got here, and I tried to neaten everything up. It's still on for breakfast tomorrow, right?" I hated lying to her.

"Absolutely, we will pick you up at nine and go out for brunch. Does that sound good?" I could hear the disappointment in her voice about tonight. She had always tried to sound enthusiastic about things, even if that wasn't how she felt. She hadn't changed at all.

It was about two o'clock; I still had about five hours before my date. "I might as well get to organizing my things," I said out loud. *Mum would be proud of me.* After about an hour, I was ironing a few things when I heard a knock on the door. "Hmm? Who could that be?" I asked out loud to no one. I glanced in the mirror, did a quick comb of my hair, and went downstairs. I walked over to the door and opened it, half expecting it to be Fiona.

"Do you always just open the door without asking who's there?" Carlos asked with a grin.

I smiled at him, "You are about four hours early; I'm not ready." I leaned against the door.

"Well, I know that, but I don't have a phone number for you, and I wanted to make our date earlier so we could go out to eat beforehand. Does five-thirty sound okay with you?" he asked me.

I glanced at my watch. "I'm not sure; it will only give me two and a half hours to get ready." I was flirting with him. "I will try, though. I don't know how great I will look in such a short amount of time," I added playfully.

"I think you look great right now, so I will expect you to be *gorgeous* when I see you next. Anyway, I have to head home; it takes me a while to get ready too." As he turned to leave, I thought of asking why he didn't introduce me to his friends but thought better of it. I waved to him and shut the door. I moaned—he was so cute—I ran upstairs to finish my ironing.

I was thrilled that I had bought some new clothes. I was almost as excited about wearing something new as I was about going on this date! So much had happened in such a short amount of time. I knew tomorrow I would have to confess to Fiona. She has been so great to me and doesn't deserve me lying to her. I am sure once I explain everything and tell her how nice Carlos is, she will approve. Who knows what will happen with my new relationship; he might be my knight in shining armor!

Five-thirty arrived before I knew it. When I heard the knock on the door, I was excited. I practically ran to open it. Just before I turned the doorknob, I hesitated and took a deep breath. *Relax.* I decided to continue the game. "Who's there?" I asked sweetly.

"The big bad wolf," he snickered as his voice went to a harsh lower register.

I opened the door and peeked around it slowly. "Hello, I like a wolf who is right on time." He growled at me while I opened the door all the way. To my surprise, he reached over to me and gave me a quick kiss on the cheek, then stepped back, waiting for a reaction from me.

My hand quickly went to the place that he kissed me. "*Oh,*" I said in surprise.

"Did I overstep some boundaries?" Carlos asked me with a pouty mouth.

" No, no, not at all. I was just surprised, that's all." I smiled at him. I looked at what he was wearing, and I hoped I was not overdressed. "Where are we going for dinner?" *He must think I am a baby.*

" It is a place called Havana Harry's. It's local. They serve just about everything, but they have great Cuban dishes."

"Am I dressed appropriately?" I asked him.

"You look awesome—just right." He smiled, grabbed my arm, and out the door we went.

The night went really great. I learned a lot of things about him and his family. His father and mother owned a small tobacco farm in Cuba. He repeated to me again that he was going back there, in the near future, for a visit. He remarked that I would love it there. I then talked about England and my family and all about my sisters and brothers. His life growing up in Cuba was very stressful. He worked very hard on his father's farm; it seemed he didn't have a fun childhood as I had; I couldn't imagine why he would want to go back there. Two years ago, a new president was appointed. His name was Fidel Castro; he was a revolutionary. I knew I wanted to find out more about this country called Cuba and this man called Fidel Castro. Perhaps I will go to the library next week to research him. I wondered if Carlos was a Communist. I would never ask him, though, because I genuinely didn't want to know.

After we finished dinner, we went to a small club. We danced and had some drinks, and no one asked for an ID from me. After a few hours, I was starting to feel a little tipsy, so Carlos suggested that we leave—I agreed with him. He helped me into the car and then went around to the driver's side and got in. We sat there for a few minutes while he stared at me.

"Are you okay?" he asked me. He moved closer towards me, put his arm around me, took my face in his hand, and kissed me. My heart began to flutter, and I felt a funny feeling in my lower body—something I had never felt before.

By the time we reached my condo, I was feeling a *little* better. I couldn't remember the last time I drank anything that strong. I apologized for having to cut our evening short and that I was having a wonderful time. He smiled at me and got out of the car, and went around to my side to help me out. He walked me up to the door, and I handed him the keys. He unlocked the door and helped me inside.

"Let me get you upstairs," he said. I nodded.

He laid me down on the bed...that is the last thing I remembered.

Chapter Eight

The bright sunlight was beaming through my bedroom window. I glanced at the clock; the time was 7:45. I put my hand up to my head and rubbed it. What had happened last night? I looked down at myself and was practically naked. *Oh, God!* I tumbled out of bed and went to the mirror; I didn't look any different. "*Oh no, no, no!* Did we...? Did I...?" I said out loud to myself, looking in the mirror. Then I remembered Fiona was picking me up at nine. I couldn't wait to jump into the shower and wash whatever I could off of my body. I hoped and prayed Carlos wasn't that kind of a guy. I then glanced at the top of my dresser; it was a note from him.

MacKenzie, don't panic; nothing happened last night. I might have brushed my hand over your body, but that was all. I took off most of your clothes because I wanted you to be comfortable. Here is my phone number. Please call me. Carlos.

Relief flooded my body. *Thank God.* I smiled as I reread his note. *He is a gentleman.* After getting dressed, I went outside to wait for my sister and decided I couldn't tell anyone about last night—no need. I will tell only *if* Carlos and I go out again. Within a short while, Don and everyone came over to pick me up. We went to a local breakfast place that served everything buffet style, and it all looked and tasted delicious—of course, we all over-ate. Afterward, Fiona suggested we drive over to the ocean to check it out. The kids were anxious to play in the water. It was a beautiful beach, and once I had my car, I would come here often.

"Mac, do you want to come back to the house for a while?" Fiona asked me.

I looked at Margo and Maria's face and thought, "How could I not say yes." They had their hands folded as if to pray. "Okay, just a few hours, though. I still have things to iron and put away."

"You are so much like Mum; it is scary." Fiona chuckled.

We all had such a wonderful afternoon at the beach and then at Fiona's home. I was amazed at how attentive Don was to Margo and Maria. They adored him. I watched with envy as the girls chased their father all over the yard; I wanted that for my life one day. We then all played badminton, and soon it was time for me to go home. Fiona and I were getting up early on Monday to pick up my car. I was so happy about that—*freedom!*

When I arrived home, I was relieved. All I could think about was calling Carlos. *Should I?* I decided I would call him; he picked up almost immediately.

"Hello?" he said.

"Hi Carlos, it's me, MacKenzie," I said softly. "I need to discuss last night with you." Before I could say anything further, he suggested he would come over to explain, or that we could meet somewhere. I hesitated a minute and then told him I would meet him at McDonald's in about ten minutes. He agreed and said he would be there in about fifteen minutes.

I really wanted him to come over, but I thought that wouldn't be appropriate because I just wanted to thank him for taking care of me and not taking advantage of me. I had to explain some things to him. He will probably think of me as an immature child; I just wanted him to know that I am not experienced in certain behavior situations. I'm sure after I tell him that, it will be over for us. *Cack!* I just realized a little English slang came out of my mouth. I grinned in the mirror as I fixed my hair.

When I crossed the street, I could see him standing outside of his car with a cigarette hanging from his lips. I don't know why, but that turned me on to those strange feelings again. *Please, God, don't let this be the end of everything.*

When he saw me, he threw his cigarette on the ground and put it out with his foot. "See," he said to me smiling, "I'm putting it out."

"I see. Good boy." I smiled back at him. I had my fingers crossed down by my side. "Carlos," I began, "I need to tell you some things and also to thank you for last night." I hesitated, "You know, putting me to bed."

"Yah, yah, I was a good boy. I will tell you I wanted you at that moment then realized you weren't that kind of a girl. You are unique. This is *Miami,* after all!"

His laugh was creepy as he reached over and grabbed me and held me. I didn't push him away even though I should have because I liked the feel of his arms around me. He then ordered me into the car—I obeyed. In a few minutes, we were both laughing at everything that had happened. I was feeling more relaxed—then told him I was a virgin!

"So, are we good?" he asked me with a twinkle in his eye.

"Did you hear what I just said?"

"Yup. I like you, MacKenzie; you are so different. We will take it as slow as you want to. I have to go to the Keys for a few days—a work thing. Let's go out on Saturday again, sound good?" He reached over and kissed me and then drove me home. "See," he said, "I won't even ask if I can come in."

I got out of the car and told him I would love to go out again with him. He seemed pleased and told me to have a good week, and he would be thinking about me when he was working. I stood outside watching as his car pulled off down the street. I watched till it vanished around the corner, then went inside and called my mother.

The next day, Fiona picked me up in the morning, and we went to pick up my first car. Frank greeted us as we pulled up. I looked around, not seeing my black BMW.

"They are just fueling up for you, Mac. We always give our customers a full tank of gas when they leave here. It is a little thing, but you would be surprised how much everyone appreciates it." Frank said, smiling. "I have all the paperwork at my desk for you to sign. We registered it for you, so as soon as you sign, you can take it home." That is what we did.

After we signed everything, I gave Frank a big hug and told him how much I appreciated his help. I knew I was fortunate to have the family I had. I also thanked Fiona. I couldn't have come to America if it wasn't for her. When they finally drove the car around to the front of the building, I couldn't believe my eyes. They had washed it and cleaned it inside and out. I practically tripped as I ran to hop in the driver's seat. Frank handed me the keys through the window. He explained a few things: like how the radio worked, windshield wipers, and air conditioning. I couldn't wait to take off on my own; I was going to head right to the mall.

Chapter Nine

When I had arrived home from the mall, I parked right in front of the building. I had a designated condo parking space for my vehicle, and all I did was stare at my car—I couldn't believe it was mine. It would be a little struggle to make payments using the money I had brought with me because it was mainly for my school supplies and to keep some aside for a place of my own someday. I knew I had to find a job. I would talk to Fiona tomorrow about her suggestion of maybe getting hired by the lawyers for which she worked.

Before I went to bed that night, I called Mum. I told her all about my new car and I also briefly mentioned Carlos. She was shocked and told me to be careful. She said she never thought I would meet someone so quickly that I really liked. Before we hung up, I had convinced her everything about him was gentlemanly. Of course, I didn't mention me getting drunk—I knew she would have freaked.

"Do Fiona and Frank like him?" she had asked before her goodbye.

I hesitated a minute. "Well, Mum, they haven't officially met him. Fiona saw him once for a brief moment, but that was it. He is away, for work, till the end of the week. I will definitely introduce him to them, don't worry." I'm not sure she was too happy, but she trusted my judgment. That night I had a dream about Carlos and me. We had married and had a big family. It was everything I had ever wanted.

The following day when I awoke, I ran to the window to make sure my car was still out front. I still couldn't believe how well everything was going. It was perfect. Now I had to concentrate on getting a job—my priority. I called Fiona at work and asked her about her firm's part-time work program for students in college. She told me she would definitely ask if they were still hiring and would get back to me.

"I will find out today and stop by your place after work. Will you be home at three?" she asked me.

My place! That sounded so unbelievable to me. "Yes, I will. See you then."

When she arrived that afternoon, she told me she had set up an interview with her boss on Thursday at ten in the morning. They needed someone to research at the library regarding a case they were working on for a special client. It sounded beautiful to me, and I was thrilled. The rest of the afternoon, we discussed girly things. I confessed to her about Carlos and said I had talked to our mother about him. I also suggested she call Mum and tell her about Don and the kids. I knew my mother would be thrilled. Fiona said that was precisely what she intended to do when she got home.

"Mac," Fiona began, "I hate to bring this up because you will think it is none of my business. I am just going to blurt it out: Are you on birth control pills or anything like that?"

I didn't see that coming, I must say. "No," I replied quickly. I didn't want to talk about it with her.

She looked surprised. "You need to make an appointment with a gynecologist and get something. I know you don't have any plans to have sex with anyone, but you never know. You can't always rely on the guy." She touched my hand. "That's all I'm going to say about the matter for now." As she fished through her bag and found her wallet, she handed me a card and said, "My gynecologist is wonderful." I took the card and thanked her, and told her I would call tomorrow and make an appointment.

"That makes me feel better," she replied. "Come over on Sunday morning and tell me all about your date, okay? I would love to meet him sometime. I will talk to you before then, though."

I was excited about my appointment with her law firm. I knew I would be going to the mall tomorrow to find some sort of a professional outfit. All I had were shorts and pants; I wanted a skirt or a dress. On Thursday, I headed over to Fiona's office for my interview. *What if I didn't get the job?* I pushed that notion immediately out of my head. Of course, I would get it; I am intelligent, reliable, and I am Fiona's sister—I was a shoo-in.

I was hired right after we finished the meeting. I would be starting on Monday—the same day I would be beginning night school. I was going to be very busy for a while. My hours were going to be nine in the morning till one in the afternoon; night school started at six p.m. *Perfect!*

Of course, I called Fiona as soon as I got home; we had a lot to talk about. She had called Mum the night before and told her everything about the kids and Don. Mum was thrilled for Fiona. They made plans for Fiona and her new family to visit England before the kids were to go back to school after the summer break—sometime in late August. I wouldn't be able to go because of school and my new job. Hopefully, I would be able to go at Christmastime.

Before I knew it, Saturday was here. I hadn't heard anything from Carlos yet. *Should I call him?* It was eight o'clock in the morning when the phone rang. My heart leaped as I picked up the phone and heard his voice.

"Do you want to take a trip with me and see some sights? We can go to the beach, out to eat, whatever you want."

"Yes, I would love to go and see some things. I have some news to tell you when I see you. What time should I be ready?" I asked him.

"Nine o'clock on the dot! See you then." He hung up and didn't give me a chance to ask him how his trip went.

I hurried and got dressed and grabbed some cereal to eat, and was all ready when he knocked on the door. As I opened the door, he grabbed me and kissed me quickly. I was shocked. "Hello," I said.

He smiled at me and said, "Let's go. I have a long day planned for us. We are taking a boat ride down the Intracoastal waterway. You will love it." He grabbed my hand, and as we got into his car, he glanced over and saw my car sitting in its parking space. "Is that your new car? It is really nice. Next time you can take *me* for a ride."

We were gone the whole day, and the Intracoastal was breathtaking. It took us past all the movie star's homes and also other millionaire's homes. I hadn't ever seen anything like it. We had a beautiful dinner on board, which I had never experienced before. We talked a lot, and he said he had missed me; I told him I wished he had called me during the week. I also mentioned my new job and that I was starting night school on Monday—I didn't want the day to end.

By the time we got back to my condo, it was late. He asked me if he could come in for a bit. I hesitated and then thought, *what the heck!* We made out on the couch, and then things started to get heavy. I already had a few drinks towards the end of the evening on the boat, and I felt the effects of it all. I was the happiest I had been in a long time, and I knew I wanted to have sex with him—I didn't want to be a virgin any longer.

So, I did something I never thought I would do. As we stood up, I grasped his hand and held it tightly while leading him towards the stairs. We looked at each other, and he asked me if I was sure. I nodded, and up we climbed.

Chapter Ten

I woke up to the sound of the phone ringing. The clock read 7:30 a.m. "Hello," I whispered while looking at Carlos, still asleep in my bed.

"Mac, are you coming over around nine for breakfast?" Fiona asked.

"Yes, yes, I will be there at nine. I just woke up. I better hurry up, talk later" I hung up the phone quickly as Carlos began to stir. He sat up and smiled at me and then patted the empty side of the bed right beside him.

"Come back to bed; it's early." I obediently went over to him and sat down. He grabbed me and kissed me.

"I, I can't," I stuttered. "That call was Fiona. I forgot I was going over there for breakfast this morning. I'm sorry," I apologized.

"No problem, I just thought last night was so spectacular, we could go another round." he grinned.

"Rain check?" I asked.

"Sure, I'll call." He quickly got out of bed, put on his pants and shirt. "I'll shower at home." The next thing I knew, he was flying down the stairs and out the door.

I got the feeling he wasn't happy with me, but what was I supposed to do? I guess his *girl*friends don't usually end their dates this quickly. I told myself I would call him later on when I got home. I jumped into the shower, got dressed, and headed out the door. As I was getting into my car, he pulled up beside me and handed me a coffee through the window.

"I forgot my kiss, and I'm sorry for taking off so abruptly. Truce?" he smiled at me.

I reached for the coffee. "Truce," I responded. We kissed, and then he turned the car around, and off he went—speeding down the road. I chuckled to myself and thought how cute he was as I took off to Fiona's house. *How much was I going to tell her?*

I spent almost the whole day with Fiona and her family. She was so lucky; Don's kids adored her. If I could find a husband as great as Don, I would be the luckiest girl in the world. They had asked me if I was nervous about starting my new job on Monday and then starting school at night. I told them I was excited about making some money and getting work experience while going to classes. No one mentioned my date with Carlos until it was time for me to leave. *Deep down, I knew I wouldn't get away without telling them of my date!*

I decided to skip the part about him sleeping over and that I was not a *virgin* any longer. I did tell them about our boat ride up and down the Intracoastal waterways. Fiona playfully hit Don and said she had never done anything that exciting. We all laughed about it, and Don said he would make plans for them to do it soon. Margo and Maria were very excited. We said our goodbyes, and Fiona told me she would see me at the office sometime tomorrow. On the drive home, I kept thinking of last night and how fantastic Carlos was about our lovemaking. He was gentle, sweet, and encouraging; I couldn't wait till we did it again. *Am I awful?*

When I arrived home, I called him immediately. He didn't answer the phone, so I left him a message to call me because I would be home the rest of the day. I was very disappointed that he wasn't home, and I knew I was falling for him. Was it love? I wasn't sure, but I had never felt this way about anyone before. I looked out the window and saw that no one was using the pool; I decided to try it out before lunch. While I was relaxing on a float, I heard someone whistle at me, and as I turned to see who it was, I flipped the float over, and Carlos began to laugh at me—what a pleasant surprise!

As the afternoon progressed, we ended up in my bedroom again. The whole afternoon we made love—I was in heaven. In the evening, Carlos wanted to take me out to dinner; I had no objections about that. We had a lovely meal and a great conversation, and I learned even more about his family and Cuba. Then he hit me with the news: He would be gone for two weeks starting this coming Tuesday.

"Why? You just got back from being away a week. Where are you going this time?" I asked him, knowing it was none of my business.

"I am going back to Cuba, as my mother is sick and I need to see her. I wish I could bring you along with me. I know you have your new job starting tomorrow and school at night. You will have plenty to keep you occupied, and I will be back before you know it," he said with a wink.

"I will miss you more than you can imagine, but you are right; I *will* be swamped for a while. " I reached out across the table and grabbed his hand. He lifted my hand and kissed it—such a gentleman.

Carlos knew not to overstay his visit, so we had an early night. He kissed me in front of my door and told me he had feelings for me that he was trying to figure out. That was how we left it. I watched him walk down the stairs and get in his car. He turned and blew me a kiss and sped down the long road before turning onto the main street. I felt sad.

The following day, I hurried my shower and picked out one of the new dresses I wanted to wear starting my new job. *Very exciting.* I was not nervous at all but couldn't figure out why I was so calm. I was very confident and was sure I would do a great job. "I got that from my dad," I thought. Mum was never sure of herself. I remembered my dad always had to assure her that she could do it right. I stood in front of the mirror and thought how professional I looked, but it was *definitely* not who I was.

When I arrived, I went immediately to my new boss's office. He welcomed me, and we sat down, and he related to me everything that would be my responsibility each day I arrived. He was working on a highly complex case and needed me to go to the library and research as far back as I could any issue similar to this particular one. He was sure there had been one or two cases like this one, and he wanted to see what the outcome had been and how it was reached.

"Yes, give me the address of the library, and I will find it," I said to him.

He smiled a big smile and replied, "I meant the law library in this building, not a regular library," he chuckled and told me it was on the second floor. "I am sure you will do a great job, Mac."

How stupid was I? "Oh, course it is. In England, a lot of the law libraries were off-site." I had hoped that sounded reasonable to him as I didn't want him to think I was stupid! As it turned out, I had a keen eye for spotting similarities in different cases—it was all fascinating to me. Within a few hours, I brought him three similar cases, all having different outcomes. He told me he was very impressed and then handed me stacks of things to put away into his file cabinets. My time flew by. Soon it was time to go home, eat, and get ready for my first night class—I barely had time to breathe.

When my night class was over, and I was home alone, I kept looking at the phone. *Why doesn't he call me?* "Maybe, I will call him," I thought as I reached for the phone and picked it up to dial; I then thought better of it and hung up. I was very disappointed he didn't even call me to say goodbye or even wish me good luck this morning before I went to work. I yawned and knew it was time to go to bed. It will be all the same things tomorrow. As I started to doze, I realized Fiona didn't even come to see me at work—no congratulations, nothing!

Chapter Eleven

It was about a week and a half after Carlos went to Cuba that I started feeling ill every morning. The first couple of days, I was just nauseous, and then I vomited before I went to work. *What was going on? Did I have a stomach bug?* It then hit me like a ton of bricks—was I... could I be...no, no, no, please, *God.* I waited till Thursday after work and stopped at the store for a test kit. Carlos would be home on Friday.

I was very embarrassed buying the kit at the store; I felt everyone was judging me, when in fact, no one really cared. At home, I read the directions *twice. While* I was waiting for the results, my mind went crazy. *I couldn't tell my mother, but I would have to tell Fiona and Frank. What would Carlos say? Would he walk away?* I had so many questions in my head it was driving me nuts! Then my timer *dinged.* I glanced over at the sink where that evil stick laid. Everything in my life was going so well, but my whole future depended on what this tiny little stick said. I was just about to reach over and look at it when my phone rang. I flew into my bedroom, picked up the phone, and said hello.

"What's the matter? You sound funny." Carlos said to me.

"Carlos? I didn't expect to hear from you till tomorrow. Did you get back early?" I didn't want to talk to anyone at this very moment—especially him.

"Yes, I just got back. I missed you. I was wondering if you wanted to get together tonight?'

"Oh. No, I am not feeling too well right now—it must have been something I ate. I'm going to bed early. We can get together tomorrow if you would like to; I don't work on Fridays, and there are no night classes either." I hoped he would understand.

"I'm sorry you aren't feeling well. I will call tomorrow morning to see if you are up to seeing me, okay?"

"That would be great, thanks; by the way, I missed you too." Finally, he hung up, and then I ran to the bathroom to see what my future held.

Pregnant! That stupid stick said my life was over! I sank to the floor, threw the stick against the door and cried. I sobbed for what seemed like hours; I had no one to blame but myself. Fiona had told me to make an appointment to see the doctor and get on some sort of birth control pill. Did I listen to her? *NO.*

After I finished my crying spell, I got up off the floor and called Fiona's doctor to make an appointment as soon as I could. I briefly explained my urgency, and they had a cancellation for the following week on Friday morning. One more week to wait. *Maybe it was a false positive.* Then I had to decide when to tell Carlos—after the doctor's appointment or before. I finally decided I would tell him tomorrow, and he can help me make some decisions that I will be facing. I am probably worrying unnecessarily.

When I woke up on Friday morning, I briefly thought I had just had a bad nightmare, and then I realized it was *real!* That nauseous feeling didn't take long to make its appearance. I spent the next few minutes on my knees, bent over the toilet, retching. I glanced over at the floor by the door and saw that awful stick. When I was sure *it* was over, I went and picked the test stick up off of the floor. Yes, it still read positive, so I tossed it into the rubbish pail. *Clunk*—it was the only thing in the rubbish.

I tried to eat something for breakfast, but I was not hungry in the least. I thought maybe I should make a cup of tea; it might settle my stomach. While sipping my tea and practicing what and how I would tell people when the time came, my phone rang. It was Carlos wanting to come over. I told him I felt better and that I had something I needed to talk to him about.

"Am I going to have to meet Fiona? I won't have a problem doing that if that's what you are concerned about," he chuckled.

"Yes, someday soon. How was your mother? You said she had been sick?" I wanted to change the subject.

"I will tell you when I get there in about an hour, okay?" I agreed, and then we hung up.

I dragged myself up the stairs, took a shower, and got dressed. This was going to be the hardest thing I would ever have to do. I prayed he would not run out the door when he found out—I knew I couldn't do this alone.

I sat on my couch waiting for Carlos to arrive, all the while practicing how I would break it to him. I was thinking: "If Carlos wanted to be in the picture, we should both go and break it to Fiona together; I wouldn't do that till after I had seen the doctor, though." The knock on the door startled me. *Well, here goes nothing!*

As I opened the door, I slowly peeked around the corner. I smiled and bowed to him while gesturing for him to enter. He bowed back and stepped in. "You're in a strange mood," he stated.

"I was trying to lighten things up a bit, but first, tell me of your trip and how your mother is doing." We sat on the couch.

"First, I want to kiss you so bad," he leaned in, and we kissed. Then he told me all about his trip. His mother had surgery, a knee replacement, and she was in a rehabilitation facility. He said he had a wonderful visit with her, and she was doing very well. Then he asked the question I was dreading.

"What did you want to discuss with me?" he asked.

"First, I want to tell you that I hope your mother will make a quick recovery, and the other news is in the upstairs bathroom rubbish." I paused as he looked confused. "Go up and look," I ordered. "Go on," I coaxed him. At least this way, I wouldn't have to say those words to him—*I'm pregnant!* The stick would do it for me.

"Is this a joke?" he smiled while looking at me as if I had gone completely *crazy!*

Up the stairs he climbed, cautiously, I might add. I waited for what seemed a long time. Then I heard the *"F"* word. I closed my eyes tightly as I heard him bound down the stairs— probably two at a time. He was holding that infamous stick!

"Is this yours?" he shouted at me.

I immediately started to cry. He just stood by the couch, holding that stick in his hand like it was a rattlesnake. Finally, he came over and sat down beside me and asked me how this could have happened, and why I would let something this crazy happen. "We have only known each other for a little over a month! I like you a lot, but..." he couldn't finish.

"I'm sorry, I really am; it was stupid of me to let this happen. If you think I wanted this to happen..." I slowly got my wits about me and told him I was scheduled to go see a doctor next week and that maybe it was a false positive. Then I added, "I am pretty sure it is positive, though, because I have been vomiting every morning since you left."

He then became very calm and told me what I didn't want to *ever* hear: "Don't worry, we can solve this problem very easily—I know someone who can make this go away." He smiled so sweetly I wanted to *slap* him.

"What?" I yelled, "*No, no, no!* I wouldn't *ever* do that to my baby. If you don't want to be a part of this, I will understand. I won't ask for anything from you." I stood up and went to the door—to show him out! That is when he rushed over to me and put his arms around me, and told me he would be there for me, and he only said that because he knew I just started a new life here and thought I would want this to go away.

"Are you absolutely sure?" I asked him. "I'm not asking for marriage or anything, so you don't have to worry." I fused into his chest. "Anyway, maybe it will be alright. Let's not worry until the doctor examines me."

"I'm going with you, okay?" he looked down at me.

My heart melted as I looked up at him. I couldn't believe that he was in this with me. It was a wonderful feeling, and I knew everything was going to be alright. Now all we had to do was tell Fiona and Frank after the doctor's visit. *That should go over big!*

Chapter Twelve

We sat together quietly, waiting to be called into the office. I held Carlos's hand so tightly as I felt him try and wiggle out of my grip. I was truly scared. I had never had a gynecological exam before. Carlos told me he would have it for me if it was possible. *Too sweet.*

"Do you have insurance?" Carlos interrupted my thoughts.

"What?" I said while quickly realizing I had some through my mother in England, but it wasn't good in another country. That was something that was on my list of things to find out, of which I never got around to doing. I hesitated, and while looking into those beautiful eyes, I said, "No, I was supposed to get some." I then explained to him about being on my mom's policy in England, but it wasn't good in this country.

"Are you kidding me?" he asked me, shocked. "How do you propose to pay for all of this?" He was clearly upset with me. It was then that I noticed his slight Cuban accent as I stared at him.

"I have some money I brought with me for school. I suppose I will have to use that." I was so ashamed of myself at this point. I wasn't going to explain to him exactly how much I had because I was instructed not to tell anyone.

He leaned in near my ear, and in a whisper, he told me to tell them we were married, and I was Mrs. Carlito Perez. He then reached into his pants pocket and took out a small wallet. "Here," he handed me an insurance card, "use this card, and as soon as we get home, I will call my insurance company and tell them I am married and to put you on my plan. I will need some information on you: date of birth, place of birth, etc."

I whispered back, "Is this legal?"

"Just do it!" he ordered, "I will explain later how it will work."

Just as I took the card from him, the receptionist called me to the desk to give her my insurance information. I turned to look at Carlos; he waved me on. *Now, I am breaking the law!*

As I was driving home, I felt Carlos's eyes on me, and we weren't saying anything to each other. I wondered what he was thinking. The doctor had confirmed our greatest fear—I was about four weeks pregnant. I had to make all my appointments for the next six months, and then depending on how things were going, he would decide whether I would come every two weeks or every week till my due date. It was a lot for me to absorb. I glanced at Carlos for some dialogue.

"Are you going to say anything? You don't have to stick around if it is too much for you."

"I told you I would be here for you. This is just not what I had planned for my life right now. I have a lot to consider, but I *will* be here for you." He reached over and grabbed my hand and squeezed tightly. "We are going to be parents!" he said, trying to be upbeat.

I started to chuckle, thinking about Fiona and Frank's reaction. I could hear them now. I suggested to Carlos he meet my sister and brother, and then we would wait about a month before telling them about the baby. It was still early, and anything could happen. I also wasn't telling my mother and other siblings about this until *much* later. He agreed with me and said he wouldn't mention it to his family until much later also. Then he suggested something that hadn't even entered my mind.

"I have a crazy idea; my brother is going back to Cuba for about a year and will be helping our parents with the farm, so I was wondering if you wanted to move in with me until the baby is born. It's a small house with two bedrooms and a big living room and kitchen. It also has a nice backyard."

I was shocked. "Do you mean it? I could help with some of the finances, and I wouldn't be in your way; I will be working and then going to school at night."

"Sounds like a plan, sweetheart. Tomorrow we will go over all the details, and I will show you the place before you really commit. It is no condo, and there is no pool. It needs some paint and sprucing up, which I will gladly do for you."

Tears welled up in my eyes as I looked at him. I didn't think he realized how much his life was about to change. When I turned into my street, he turned and told me he wasn't going to stay as he was supposed to meet some friends a little later. I said I understood and realized that we both had to have some time to sort things out. I wanted to be alone anyway. We made plans for tomorrow morning for breakfast. He gave me a kiss, got into his car, and left. He honked the horn as he started down the long driveway. As I watched him leave, I rubbed my stomach. *What if he never comes back?* Because it was so hot outside, I decided to take a swim to relax a little bit. *Was this a bad dream?*

I went into the house and made a little something to eat; I changed into my bathing suit, all the while wondering how long I would be able to wear it. When I went to jump into the water, I noticed there was a woman, who had to be about six or seven months pregnant, relaxing in the shallow end. I dove in and swam to where she was and started a conversation with her—I desperately needed a friend besides Fiona to talk to about being pregnant.

Her name was Jessica, and her husband's name was Dan. They had been married for a few years, and he was in the Air Force and was currently stationed overseas. She welcomed my friendship, especially when I told her I was pregnant. I mentioned that I was not married to the father and hoped one day that would happen, but I wasn't going to pressure him. We bonded almost immediately, and I told her briefly my story of how I came to America and why. She said she was from Arizona and met her husband there. The last few years, she traveled with him to wherever he was stationed, and then she got pregnant, and they decided to buy the condo because she wouldn't be going overseas with him. She was twenty-three years old, and they just celebrated their second anniversary.

"It's been lonely here by myself," she said, "most of the people who live here are a little older than I am. Dan has one more year to go, and he will be done."

I liked her immediately, and I knew we would be good friends. I will try and look at the positive side. Pregnancy, after all, doesn't mean a death sentence! *I can do this.*

Chapter Thirteen

I went out to eat with Carlos the next morning. I chatted about my new friend I had met at the pool after he left the previous night. I mentioned that she and her husband were expecting in a few months; I also threw in the fact they had been married for a few years and were very happy—the emphasis on *happy! It wouldn't hurt if I threw some hints out there.* I wasn't sure he was really listening to me because he was eating like there was no tomorrow.

"Hurry up, Mac, I want to show you my place. We can then go over to Fiona's house, and you can properly introduce me. How does that sound?" he asked.

"Yes, I can't wait till I see the house, and we can stop by Fiona's house afterward to see if they are home." I tried to sound excited, but it just wasn't happening, and I didn't know why.

His house was about five miles from Fiona's condo. As he drove into the driveway, I scanned the neighborhood. It wasn't what I was used to, that's for sure. I didn't think Florida had any neighborhoods that were on the poorer side, but I guess they do.

"This is cute," I said to him. "It just needs a little tender loving care," I added.

"You don't like it, I can tell." He turned the motor off and sat for a minute, and then replied, "Well, let's get this over with. I don't know how else we are going to do this. Do you want to live together?" he said as he turned to look at me.

"Yes, of course, I do. It's just not the Green Gables!" As soon as that came out of my mouth, I regretted it.

"Green Gables is temporary—this is permanent. My brother and I own it. I can work on it when I have some spare time, and with some fresh paint and some yard work, it will look better."

He was trying, and I was a spoiled, privileged woman. "I'm sorry," I said to him. "You are right; this will work; we will make it work. Thank you for this."

As we walked through the front door, I immediately could envision two bachelors living here. It wasn't the cleanest. There were dirty dishes here and there and signs of smoking *something* in the ashtrays—definitely not cigarettes. Carlos immediately started to pick up the dishes while making excuses as to why things were so messy. I went over to him and put my arms around him.

"Stop cleaning everything up; finish showing me the rest of the house, and maybe after work tomorrow, I can come over and begin a good cleaning till I have to go to my class." I smiled at him and then kissed him. I could feel him relaxing. After the tour, I could definitely feel the potential in the house. I wondered what Fiona would think! She would not be happy about *anything* I was about to do.

On the drive over, I was secretly hoping no one would be home. I didn't want to tell Fiona where I would be living for the next several months— maybe longer. I looked at Carlos, and he didn't seem to be worried at all. When we pulled into their driveway, Margo and Maria ran down from the front steps yelling my name. They were very excited to see me.

"Mac, who is driving your car?" Margo asked, pointing at Carlos.

"A friend of mine, his name is Carlos," I told her. Maria just stood quietly. She was the shy one.

"Oh, he is cute. Hi Carlos." she smiled.

"Go get mom for me, will you?" I asked her. She quickly turned and ran into the house. Within seconds Fiona came out of the house and invited us both inside. I told her we were out, and so I thought this would be a good time to introduce Carlos to everyone. Fiona looked at me and then at Carlos. I knew she thought that he was too old for me. Fiona mentioned Don was not at home because he was working. She explained to Carlos that Don was a nurse at the hospital and had screwy hours. She was pleasant to him.

"I think Mac mentioned to me that he was a nurse," Carlos stated.

"Would you guys like something to drink or eat?" she asked us. "Please have a seat."

I was anxious to get this visit over with. The exchange back and forth of pleasantries between the two of them was enough to make me retch. How was I going to tell her now about my moving in with him? I decided I would do it when I was alone with her—in a few days. Fiona invited us to supper, so I quickly made up an excuse that I had some things I still wanted to do before going home. Carlos looked at me confused but was smart enough to know I wasn't going to tell her today. After playing with the kids for a few minutes and talking about nothing important, we made our exit. As we were leaving, Fiona made sure we promised to come back in a few days and stay for dinner. We promised we would, and then I kissed the girls, and off we went.

On the way home, Carlos looked at me and asked, "What was that all about? I thought you were telling her you were moving in with me."

"Trust me," I said. "It was not the right time; she was just being polite to you. I could see the wheels turning in her head. It is better if I do it when you are not around. I will tell her tomorrow after work."

"I thought we were getting on pretty well. I thought she liked me." he smiled at me while he rolled his eyes.

We both started to laugh and headed for the condo. That night we made love and then he went home. It was an exhausting day for me. I never did tell Fiona I was moving out until *after* I had moved. Carlos and I went over for dinner as we planned about a week after I moved out. I will just say—it didn't go well. She had the girls go up to their rooms, and we all went into the living room. That is when she let me have it: I was too young, I was stupid, childish, crazy, and then she lit into Carlos after she found out he was six years older than me. To tell you the truth, I didn't know he was twenty-four. While we were being reamed out, I quietly told her that I was pregnant. She stood up and asked us to leave. She wanted to be alone and couldn't believe what I had just told her. I tried to explain, but she wouldn't hear me out. If she had a gun, I knew she would have shot Carlos. We left quietly.

Chapter Fourteen

We spent the next several months sprucing up the house with new paint outside and inside. I had a lot of fun picking out colors for each room. I was getting bigger and bigger by the day, and in a few weeks, we would become parents. Somehow Carlos always managed to pay for all the repairs and changes that were made. Once in a while, he would be gone for a week—work-related. One day, I decided to ask him what he did when he was away. He never spoke about his work, but it seemed to pay very well. He always seemed to evade my questions, changing the subject to the house or about the baby. Finally, after making love one night and being in a very good mood, I brought up the subject of what he exactly did when he went to the Keys. He looked at me and then began his explanation after first making me promise not to tell anyone what he was about to confide in me. Of course, I promised, what choice did I have—I wanted to know!

"As you know," he began, "most of the time I work on the docks, loading and unloading ships; then there are times when I try to help people get into America, mostly from Cuba." He stared at me.

"What do you mean? Helping people how? Smuggling them into the country illegally?" I was in a little bit of a shock.

"Yes, but America's relationship with Cuba, as you must know, is strained, to say the least. People want to come to America to live. So, I smuggle them in, give them passports, and a place to live."

"And..." I responded.

"I get paid very well." He then stomped off and went outside.

I felt the baby kick. I was feeling ill, and I didn't know what to do. What if he got caught? I went to the window to see where he was. He was swinging on a swing set he had bought right after we moved in. He looked so unhappy. What I couldn't understand was, why did he want me to bring the baby to Cuba so his parents could meet their grandchild? How would we get there—smuggle us in? What would happen if we couldn't get back? I promised him a while ago we would go to Cuba when the baby was old enough. Maybe things would be different by then. I had asked him why he loved Cuba so much; he replied because of the countryside and the people. He told me that Cuba was misunderstood by the world, and his people didn't like Fidel Castro either, but someday things would change.

"I will never give up hope for my country." he once told me.

I had to lie down; my head felt like a jackhammer was demolishing it. At this late stage of my pregnancy, I didn't care what popped into my mouth. I needed something strong to stop this hammering! I must have fallen asleep because the next thing I knew, Carlos was shaking me awake. I could smell something cooking on the stove.

"Are you hungry?"

I shook my head and told him I wasn't feeling very well. The baby was kicking so hard that I thought it would break through my stomach wall. I looked at the panic that was on Carlo's face and quickly reminded him it was too early for the baby to come. He helped me off the couch, and that is when my water broke! *Oh no!*

Carlos immediately called the doctor and then left a message for Fiona to meet us at the hospital. We were on our way within minutes. The pains started coming closer and closer together. In my head, I knew that this would be the last time I would ever be *pregnant.* I tried panting like I was taught at our classes—not helping! Girl or Boy was all I could concentrate on. We hadn't decided on any name yet because we thought we would have more time.

When I began to moan very loudly, Carlos grabbed my hand and squeezed it tightly. When we arrived, a staff of two nurses was waiting outside with a wheelchair. I was whisked away quickly, and Carlos was told to go to the waiting room; they would let him know and not to worry, I would be fine. I thought I heard Carlos yelling to me that he loved me—he had better!

One doctor checked me, and I heard him tell the nurse that I was fully dilated. They turned to me and told me *not* to push yet while I was being put on a gurney. I was in so much pain; there was nothing to compare with this. I begged them to give me something to ease the pain. Finally, I felt I was drifting in and out. I heard them tell me to push a couple of times and that I was doing wonderfully. *Was I?*

The next thing I knew, I was being handed this beautiful baby. I was very groggy but heard the word *boy*. I cried more because this was finally over than the fact, I finally had my son.

As I held him and looked at his tiny hands in his mouth, I couldn't believe it. I then looked at the door and saw Carlos, Fiona, and Frank trot in, grinning from ear to ear.

"You did it," Fiona said. Frank leaned in and kissed me and said he was so proud of me. They then had to make room for Carlos. He kissed me and thanked me for giving him a son. The nurse took him away from my hold and gave him to Carlos. His smile was a mile long.

"I want to introduce you to Carlos Perez Jr. He is so beautiful," he said to everyone.

Fiona and I glanced at each other. "Mac," she said to me, "Didn't you want to name him John, after dad?" I hesitated.

"Carlos, can we talk about the name?" That was a cue for Fiona and Frank to leave. They told me they would be back a little later. I turned to Carlos and looked at him with some disappointment in my eyes.

"What is there to talk about? A boy is always named after their father in Cuba."

"Well, this isn't Cuba," I said quietly. "I wanted John for his name, and we could call him Johnny while he was small." Then I quickly added, "Carlos can be his middle name."

"How about if Carlos is his first name and John is his middle name!"

I was tired, and so I agreed, but I said that we would call him Johnny while he was young. Carlos finally agreed to that, and I was relieved. He then shocked me when he told me I must sign the birth certificate as Mrs. Carlos Perez or the insurance would not pay for anything.

"I know it seems illegal, but it is what we have to do. Do you think all your prenatal visits would have been paid had you not said we were married?"

I knew I should refuse, but who would be responsible for all the expenses if I didn't do it his way? So, I agreed. *Does Carlos ever do anything legally?*

Chapter Fifteen

The next six months were a big adjustment for both of us. I will say Carlos was the perfect dad. Everyone who saw him with Johnny said so. You could tell he was very proud and loved him very much. We were okay but not perfect. We had different ideas about what to do about certain things. I had spoken to my mother a few weeks after he was born. She was disappointed in me but couldn't wait till I sent her pictures of him—her first grandchild! I said we would visit England as soon as we could. Carlos kept mentioning that we had to go to Cuba to show his parents soon. I agreed and told him I had to wait for a good time to ask for a vacation from the firm where I was working at night—I was stalling.

I did so well at Fiona's firm that when I received my diploma from night school, they hired me. They knew I was going to have a baby and would probably be taking a little leave but kept me on anyway at night—it was working out. Carlos babysat when I was at work, and if he had to go for a week, then Fiona would do the sitting. She loved Johnny very much, and Maria and Margo were a great help.

Fiona still wasn't crazy about Carlos but admitted he was a great father and truly loved his son. She spoke to me one day and said she didn't trust Carlos. I just listened to her suspicions, but of course, I already knew that he was doing illegal activities. I felt she had no reason not to like him, as he bent over backward to try to get her to accept him; she kept telling me there was something about him, but she couldn't put her finger on it. I hoped she would never find out the truth about what he was doing.

One day, out of the blue, Fiona and Don came over and asked if I could get away for a weekend and go to Disney World with all of them since I had yet to go there. I was excited and then asked if Johnny was too young to go. Fiona suggested to Carlos that he could perhaps watch Johnny for two days.

"Mac could get away and do something she has wanted to do her whole life, and it would be more fun if she didn't have to worry about the baby." Carlos smiled at her.

"I have been there a few times, so of course I wouldn't mind," he said, glancing at me.

I think he knew it would be hard for me to go somewhere without my *pumpkin,* as I called him. "Are you sure you will be alright, Carlos? It is not easy, you know."

"Yes, I will be fine. I want to teach him some Spanish anyway," he said, trying to get a rise out of Fiona, "for when we go to Cuba to meet his grandparents." he added.

Fiona looked wide-eyed at me, and I knew she wanted more information but kept her mouth shut. I would explain later to her. We decided on two weeks from now. I was very grateful to Carlos and excited to be able to finally experience Disney World. After everyone left, I asked Carlos that when Johnny was a little older, perhaps just the three of us could go there. He was immediately on board with that idea.

"Just the three of us!" he said. He then said he keeps trying to warm up to Fiona, but it wasn't working. I went over to him and hugged him.

"She will come around, Carlos. She is just overprotective of me. I am her baby sister. I don't think she would warm up to anyone I was with; it's not you personally." I lied. I looked at the playpen where Johnny was snoozing peacefully. "Look at what we made," I said to Carlos. "I think he looks just like you." I knew he would lap that up.

Two weeks flew by, and before I knew it, I was packing an overnight bag. I would be leaving in the morning. Could I really leave my *Pumpkin* for two whole days? Carlos sensed my hesitation and immediately put his arms around me and said Johnny would be in good hands. The next morning Fiona came to the door; she wanted to give Johnny a kiss goodbye and also thank Carlos again for taking this on. She thought maybe she had misjudged him. I ran and got my camera before we left; I wanted Fiona to take a picture of Carlos, me, and Johnny. We had lots of pictures of Johnny, Carlos and Johnny, and me and Johnny but none of the three of us together, just the picture Fiona took when I had first delivered him. I gave Johnny a million kisses and told him not to forget me. Carlos rolled his eyes at Fiona. Fiona shrugged her shoulders. I turned to Carlos and gave him a big kiss and whispered in his ear that I knew I was overreacting. He smiled while picking up Johnny. He took Johnny's little hand and made him wave to me. "Say goodbye to mommy." He grinned while I walked out the door.

Disney World was like no other place I had ever been before. It was awe-inspiring. We had a fabulous time. I think Fiona thought she had three children instead of two. Maria, Margo, and I were inseparable. I liked every ride they liked, even the childish rides. That first night, after the girls fell asleep, Fiona asked the dreaded question I was hoping she wouldn't ask.

"Are you planning to take Johnny to Cuba? That place is a Communist country! America is always having problems with Castro. Have you read up on this place? If not, you need to do it."

I had to calm her down and tell her that I had not planned to go to Cuba, at least not until things got better over there. She was not to worry. I wouldn't put Johnny in harm's way—ever! I explained that I never say no completely to Carlos; I just keep making excuses as to why we can't go right now. I so wanted to tell her about how Carlos is trying to help his people have a better life in America, but I am sure that would push her into the deep end.

In the morning, we went back to Disney and spent half a day there, and then headed home. I was anxious to see Johnny and, of course, Carlos. This little vacation was exactly what I had needed, though. Taking care of a baby and working nights was very difficult, even with help from Carlos. I had taken lots of pictures and couldn't wait to get them developed.

It took us four hours to drive home, and I was glad I didn't have to drive all that way. I was exhausted. They dropped me off in front of my house. We all kissed and hugged and promised to get together soon. I waved until I could no longer see the car as it disappeared around the last turn. What a great time I had.

I don't know why I had an uneasy feeling when I opened the door and walked in. No one was there to greet me. I called out that I was home. Silence! "Carlos, are you home?" I slowly walked into Johnny's bedroom—*everything was gone!* I looked in the closet; his clothes were all gone. I quickly went to his bureau, nothing! I ran into our room and opened Carlo's bureau drawers one by one. *Panic* set in! I slid down the wall and screamed as loud as I could, "What did *he* do?"

Part TWO

"Scott"

Chapter Sixteen

It had been two years since I last saw my precious *pumpkin*, Johnny. Carlos and Johnny seemed to have vanished into thin air. The house the three of us lived in, as it turned out, didn't belong to Carlos and his brother. Carlos was house-sitting while the owners were visiting relatives for a couple of years in Europe. I met Sgt Scott Thomas when he was working on my case—trying to find Carlos and Johnny. The detective assumed he went back to Cuba, but because of our bad relationship with that Communist country, he received no help from their authorities. The Sgt. promised me they would never give up trying to find them both. Scott, as he wanted me to call him, told me since Carlos had Johnny's birth certificate and I had signed a false name, it would be a very difficult task. The department was pretty sure Carlos Perez was not his real name. I was constantly in contact with the Miami police and all the detectives involved. It could be considered a second-degree felony charge if they could find him because I had told the authorities Carlos would never harm his son. He loved him very much.

These last two years, for me, have been the most horrible, stressful, and unimaginable time in my life. I prayed every day that Carlos would walk through my door with our son. Why wouldn't he, at least, send me a picture or write a letter to let me know Johnny was okay, as he must realize what I am going through. I am now under a therapist's care because, at one point, I was suicidal, but I was made to realize that I need to stay positive and strong. Someday, Johnny might come back to me. Every night I look at the picture of Carlos, Johnny and myself, that was taken before I went to

Disney World with Fiona and her family. It is inconceivable I could be so happy and excited one minute and devastated the next—*it was a nightmare!*

I am sitting in my bedroom looking into the mirror. I am waiting for Fiona to come over to help me get dressed for my wedding—I would soon become Mrs. Scott Thomas. We started dating during the investigation, and now I am *with child*—Fiona's expression, not mine. When I told Scott about the baby, he seemed happy. Right away, he asked me to marry him; I didn't hesitate at all. I couldn't do this alone, and I was determined to do it the right way this time. Do I love him? I'm not sure. Fiona and Frank are crazy about Scott, so since I am not a good judge of character, I decided they knew what was best for me. What is love anyway?

In three hours, I would be married and on my way to the Bahamas. It was a place I would never have gone to if I had been single. Scott had a very good job working as a detective for the Miami Police Department, and he was kind, attentive, and I knew he loved me. My only problem was that his job was very dangerous. I had heard many horror stories of detective's wives becoming young widows. Of course, he always assured me that nothing like that would ever happen to me.

"I take all the precautions, and I never do anything foolish," he used to say to me. "So, don't worry, Miss Mac," as he liked to call me.

One night when we were together, he told me he had only been shot at once in his short career. *Was that supposed to make me feel better?* I think that was the night I got pregnant! Every time I think of that time, I have to laugh; he really is a good guy. A knock on the door brought me back to reality. It must be Fiona. I ran downstairs and opened it.

"Hello Mac, sorry to disturb you. I just wanted to wish you all the best and have a great honeymoon," Kelly said as she handed me an envelope.

Kelly was a friend and neighbor I had met recently. She lived in the complex with her husband also. Scott and I decided we would stay in Fiona's condo and pay her rent. It would be plenty big for the three of us, and it really was in a beautiful, well-kept area. Scott said it probably wouldn't be forever, but for now, it was perfect. I thanked Kelly for her thoughtfulness and told her we would get together when Scott and I got back from the Bahamas. We hugged, and just as she was leaving, Fiona pulled into the driveway. She waved to Kelly as she got out of her car.

"Everything OK?" Fiona asked.

I explained to her that Kelly wanted to wish me well and had given me an envelope. I opened it and found a check inside of a beautiful card. "That was very nice of her; she didn't have to do that," I told her.

"Well, let's get started on your hair," she said as her fingers ran through the back of my head. "Such a job this will be, but I will make it work." At that comment, we proceeded up the stairs to my room.

Fiona worked on my hair and makeup. "I looked gorgeous," I thought to myself.

"Fiona, you could have been a successful hairdresser. Look at me!" I smiled at her. "Thank you for doing this. Is it too early to put on my dress?" I asked her.

"No," she said. "Where is it?" she asked as she went to the closet.

"It is downstairs hanging up in the kitchen," I said. Then I started to sneeze. "Bring up a box of Kleenex on the counter, will you?" I asked as Fiona headed for the stairs.

"I have some in my purse; also, Mum sent her beautiful necklace that Dad had given her on their wedding day. It's in my purse also."

I walked over to her purse that was lying on my dresser. I saw the box the necklace was in. I carefully opened it. Wow! It was the most beautiful necklace I had ever seen, with so many diamonds. I don't remember my mother ever wearing it, though; it would be something I borrowed. I pulled out a Kleenex and blew my nose. "I better not be coming down with a cold," I thought. I then noticed an envelope tucked away in the corner of her bag. Curiosity got the better of me, and I grabbed it quickly, thinking it was a present for me. I looked at the envelope, and it was addressed to Fiona. Something about the writing made me shiver throughout my body. I had to open it. There was no return address, and it had already been opened. The only thing in the envelope was a picture of a small boy about two years old. I immediately knew who it was!

This is my wedding day! I put the picture back in the envelope and placed it inside of my dresser drawer. I would deal with Fiona later. I had a wedding to attend, and I needed to be happy!

All during our ceremony and the reception, I couldn't stop thinking of that picture. Whenever Fiona caught me staring at her, she always smiled. Of course, I smiled back, but I wondered what she knew about Johnny's whereabouts. That photo *had* to be of Johnny—his eyes and mouth were the same as I remembered, and that little boy was about the same age as Johnny would be now. If I find out that Fiona knew something all this time about his disappearance, I don't know what I will do to her. Why wouldn't she let me know if Carlos had reached out to her? There were so many questions I needed to ask her, but this was not the time. When Scott and I reach the Bahamas, maybe I will tell him what I had found.

Scott and I said our final goodbyes as we were hugging and thanking everyone who had attended. When I reached Fiona, I politely hugged her and whispered into her ear that we had to have a talk when I came back from the honeymoon! *Was that a frightened look on her face?*

Chapter Seventeen

Flying home from the Bahamas, I was thinking of the last five days. They were perfect. I had decided not to mention anything about Johnny to Scott. I wanted to wait until we were back in the condo—nothing was going to ruin our honeymoon! Scott was acting funny; he actually wouldn't let me walk into the house. To my surprise, he picked me up and carried me over the threshold.

"*Oh my*," I said, shocked. "I thought this was only done in the movies." He continued carrying me up the stairs without a word and laid me down gently on our bed. I knew what was coming next—or so I thought.

"I love you, Miss Mac," he said as he kissed me. "Is there something wrong because you have had a faraway look in your eye since the wedding. Do you have regrets?" He began to rub my stomach gently. "I can't wait till this baby is born. Are you thinking of Johnny?" he asked as he began to remove my clothing.

I couldn't believe how observant he was. Being a detective, though, it made perfect sense that he would pick up on small things. He was trained to be able to tell when someone was not telling the truth, or they were holding something back. I think it is time to come clean.

"You're right about me not being there fully at the wedding and even on our honeymoon. I *have* been thinking of Johnny." He then put his finger to my lips to quiet me.

"Tell me afterwards. At this moment, I want you so badly."

Then we made love for the first time as Mr. and Mrs. Scott Thomas in our home.

We laid in each other's arms, and I was at peace because I had finally found what I had been wanting. I was married and about to have my second child. After a few minutes, I sat up quickly and got out of the bed, then went to my dresser and took out the envelope I had hidden. I turned slowly and looked at Scott lying on the bed with his eyes closed. "Here," I said, handing him the envelope.

He sat up, startled. "What is this?" he asked nervously as he opened it up and pulled out the picture of Johnny? "Who's this?" he asked as he looked at the address on the envelope.

"I'm pretty sure it is Johnny; I took the envelope out of Fiona's purse the day of our wedding when she came over to do my hair. I thought it was a wedding card for us. She must realize it is missing by now."

"This is key evidence in our case. It was postmarked two weeks ago from Coral Gables to your sister. It was mailed from here!" He quickly got out of bed and started to pick up the phone. I stopped him.

"Not today, please. I need to talk to her first. *Please.*" He looked at me and put the receiver down. "Thank you," I said. "I will talk to her tomorrow and find out what is going on, Okay? We just came back from our honeymoon; let me have this day before it all comes rushing back to me again—the heartache."

I woke up before Scott and quietly got dressed as I didn't want to wake him. I had to think about what I was going to say to Fiona. *How could she keep something like this from me?* I started down the stairs, tip-toeing as I went.

"Miss Mac, come back to bed!" Scott yelled loudly.

I quickly continued down the stairs like I hadn't heard him and went into the kitchen. *Please don't come down.* After a few minutes, he appeared in the kitchen. He came over towards me and grabbed and kissed me.

"Good morning, Mrs. Thomas," he said affectionately.

"You should have stayed in bed," I responded after our kiss. "Do you want some breakfast?"

"Boy, you're grumpy this morning. Is this what you're like in the morning?"

I smiled at him and explained I needed some time to think about how I was going to approach Fiona about the picture. "I can imagine how she will react to my stealing an envelope out of her purse," I told him.

"Well, *you* did it; that isn't the problem, though. She was keeping important information from you and the police—that's a problem for me. Do you want me to go with you?"

"*No!*" I said emphatically. "I need to do this on my own—hear what she has to say before I *kill* her.

Scott grinned, then looked worried. "This is a side of you I've never encountered. Remind me never to cross you. If looks could kill..."

"And just remember this look," I said playfully, pointing my finger in his face. I grabbed the picture, my purse, and keys as I turned to blow him a kiss while walking out the door.

While driving over to her house, I practiced what I would say to her. Should I remain calm or start in as a raving maniac? I was plenty angry and wasn't sure how I would do it; I pulled into the driveway and came to an abrupt halt. I knew Don would be at work, the kids were at school, and she had this day off, so no matter how I reacted when I looked at her smiling face, no one would hear anything that I said to her. I walked up to the door and just walked in.

"Fiona!" I yelled for her.

She came immediately around the corner, wiping her hands on a towel. "Welcome ba..." she stopped when she saw my face. "What's the matter?"

I reached into my bag and pulled out the picture that I thought was Johnny. "*This*" I shoved the picture into her face. She looked at the picture in horror and quickly went to her bag that was lying on the couch. She began frantically pushing things around inside. "Don't bother looking in there. I found it when I went into your purse on the day you did my hair. Remember I took out a Kleenex and our mother's necklace?" I tried to control the tone of my voice.

"Mac, calm down; I can explain everything." She went and sat on the sofa, and I sat on the chair opposite her.

"Just answer me this one thing; Is this Johnny?" I was livid. Immediately, Fiona started to cry. "Stop the weeping act, Fiona, and answer my question, or I swear I will call the police right now!"

Fiona stammered and stuttered a few minutes and then calmly replied. "Yes, it is. I have another one I received last year when he was a year old. I swear I don't know who sent it or why they sent it to me." she began twisting the towel over and over again.

Remaining calm, I said just above a whisper, "Why didn't you tell me?"

"I didn't want to bring up all the sadness again for you. I thought seeing these pictures would just hurt you even more." Fiona got up off the couch and came over to me, kneeling in front of my chair. "Please, Mac, forgive me." She begged. "At least we know he is okay, wherever he is."

I began to respond slowly. "You realize this is or could have been an important clue. It is postmarked *here*. You realize I have to tell Scott and he will give this picture and the first one to the police. Please get the other one for me." I could hardly look at her. She immediately left to retrieve the other photo.

Then the pain hit me; I doubled over in agony.

Chapter Eighteen

The next thing I remembered was being rushed into an exam room at the hospital, followed by two nurses and a doctor asking me questions. "Where's Scott?" I yelled out. One of the nurses said he was out in the hall, and I could see him after my examination. "Is my baby all right?" I asked frantically.

"That is what we are going to check," said the doctor. He began to throw out orders to the two nurses and then briefly left the room. When he returned, he checked me thoroughly, then told me I wasn't in labor, and the baby's heartbeat was strong. He said it was false labor known as Braxton Hicks. I was so relieved. I asked him if stress could have brought on this episode and if it could happen again.

"Possibly, and it may happen again, but don't stress about it. You have a few months to go before it is for real." He then patted my knee as he left. A few minutes later, Scott and Fiona came into the room.

"I was so worried about you, Mac. When Fiona called me, I was frantic." Scott said to me as he walked over to kiss me. "The doctor said you could get dressed and go home."

I couldn't even look at Fiona; I basically ignored her. The nurses then told them to step out of the room so I could get dressed. I was relieved. Thankfully that pain had subsided, and I was going home—I was exhausted. Scott said he would go and get the car and pull it around to the front. A nurse made me sit in a wheelchair as we headed to the front of the hospital. Fiona was very quiet but held my hand as I was wheeled down the hall to the door. She opened the car door and helped me into the front seat. She said her car was in the emergency parking lot and she would call me tomorrow. I quietly told her not to bother. I think she pretended not to hear me as she leaned in and kissed me on my cheek.

On the way home, Scott made small talk and asked me if I was hungry. He then asked about Fiona. "What happened when you went over Fiona's house? You were pretty rude to her today; what did she tell you about the picture?"

I knew I didn't want to get into it tonight, so I told him I was tired and a little hungry and was going to bed as soon as I ate something. I looked at him as he was driving. "Scott, I have something to tell you, but I don't want to do it today. We will talk tomorrow, okay? Will you be able to stay home tomorrow?"

He turned to glance at me. "Of course, I will call in. Should I be worried?"

"No," I told him. "I'm just overwhelmed right now. I found out something that is important but nothing for you to worry about now." He seemed okay with that explanation.

Soon we were home, and when I was sitting on the sofa, Scott was fussing over me, which felt really nice. He prepared something for me to eat and then made me put my feet up on the coffee table. I smiled at him.

"Do you want to take a nap afterward?" he asked me. He knew it had been a long and emotional day. If only he knew how truly emotional this day was for me.

"No, I will just go to bed early. Sit with me, and let's watch a movie together."

For the next few hours, we watched TV while holding each other—it was nice. After the movie, I told him I was going to bed, and he said he had a few things to do and would be up soon. We kissed, and I proceeded up the stairs by myself. When I reached the top of the stairs, I quickly realized I had left my bag on the floor in the living room, so I turned to head back down the stairs. Suddenly, I stopped halfway down because Scott was on the phone talking to someone. Her name was Anna!

"Anna? Who was *she?"* I wondered—no one I had ever heard about. When I walked into the room, Scott quickly said to the person he was speaking to that he would talk tomorrow. Should I let on that I overheard some of their conversations? Instead, I told him I wanted my bag next to the sofa. He quickly went over and grabbed it for me.

"I will be up in a minute, Miss Mac," he replied with a smile, handing me my purse.

Did he seem a little nervous? *"Oh, stop it, MacKenzie,"* I said to myself. It had been a very long day, and I couldn't wait to take a shower and get into my nightclothes. While I was in the shower, I heard him come up the stairs. The next thing I knew, he was in the shower with me.

"I figured I would save water," he smirked and winked at me. "I called the precinct and told them I wouldn't be in tomorrow. We will have the whole day to do anything you feel like doing," he added.

I wasn't feeling *it,* I told him quietly. He quickly let go of me and said he understood. We finished our shower, and I got out first, wrapped a towel around myself, and went into our bedroom to put on my nightclothes; he remained in the shower longer. I crawled into bed, snuggled under my comforter, and after several minutes, I heard Scott head downstairs. I thought about what our conversation would be like in the morning as I drifted slowly off to sleep.

It was quite late in the morning when I woke up. I glanced at the clock, and it read 9:30 a.m. I wondered what time Scott had gone to bed or if he even had. His side of the bed looked like no one had slept there. *Did he sleep downstairs?* I went to the top of the stairs and called down to him. I heard him yell to come down—breakfast was ready. I put on my robe and grabbed the picture and envelope I had of Johnny, and slowly went quietly down to the kitchen. *What would I say?*

"Good morning, sunshine," he said as he pointed to the chair that he wanted me to sit on.

I reached into the pocket of my robe and pulled out the picture and envelope, and held it in my lap. I waited till he served me my eggs and bacon and sat down himself before I mentioned to him that Fiona had another picture of Johnny besides this one; it was when he had turned one.

"Do you have that picture also?' he was getting angry.

"I do not have it with me." Before he could say anything further, I continued. "Someone sent this picture to Fiona after his second birthday. He or she also sent her a picture of him on his first birthday last year." I waited for his reaction.

After a few minutes, he replied, *"What!* Has she had *two* pictures with envelopes in her possession for over a year? Oh boy, you go upstairs and get dressed; we are going to pay her a visit!"

Chapter Nineteen

We rode in silence all the way over to Fiona's house. I was pretty sure she only worked three days at the beginning of the week but sometimes on Saturdays. It was a beautiful fall Friday morning in Florida—very warm with little humidity. It was a shame that in a few minutes, it would all go to hell! For a couple of minutes, which seemed like an eternity, we sat in her driveway contemplating what we would say and how to say it.

"I think I should speak first, okay?" I said to Scott. Reluctantly he agreed. I knew he was very upset with Fiona. The next thing I knew, we were knocking on her front door.

When she opened the door, she looked very surprised to see us both standing there. "I see you are feeling okay now." Directing her comment to me alone, not even looking at Scott.

"Fiona, we need to talk to you about your pictures of Johnny. May we come in?" I was very polite to her—Scott said nothing. She gestured with a wave of her hand to come in.

"Can I get you both something? I just brewed some fresh coffee." We politely declined and told her we had already eaten our breakfast and had coffee.

Following her into the living room, we took a seat on the couch, and she sat opposite us in a rather large overstuffed recliner. I thought she looked so tiny sitting in it—like a child. I started speaking first. "Do you have that other picture of Johnny when he was one?" I then took out the picture I had and handed it to Scott. Fiona got up and went into her small office, and came back with the picture. I waited a few seconds, thinking she would say something, then she handed it to Scott. Everything was so formal, not like it used to be. We were always so close.

Scott took both photos and put them in a plastic bag he had brought with him. He did it very carefully so as not to put any more finger marks on the photos. I must have looked a little confused because he explained to us about fingerprints that may be on the photos, which could be a lead. I think it dawned on Fiona the importance of showing the photos to us as soon as she had received them.

"I am so sorry, Mac; I was trying to protect you." She then looked directly at Scott. "I hope you don't think I knew anything about Carlos's plan to kidnap Johnny?" She was shaking.

"Fiona, I don't know anything for sure. All I know is you had some important evidence that you held onto. I would like you to come down to the station today, if possible, to make a formal statement. There may be some questions my superiors want to ask you. Can you come today? It won't take too long. I will go with you, and you're not in trouble." he told her calmly.

After agreeing, Fiona and Scott got into her car. I couldn't look at her for very long, and I knew she understood why I didn't go with them. Scott gave me a quick kiss and said they wouldn't be gone too long and to go home because Fiona would take him back to the condo when they were through.

All the way home, I kept thinking back to when we had gone to Disney World. What I was pretty sure of was that Fiona hated Carlos. She had suspicions about him early on in our relationship. I remembered she told me she just didn't trust him. I really didn't think she was involved, and what she told us about protecting me against further heartache, I believed. I decided she just made a wrong judgment call. *Who hadn't done that!*

When I arrived home, I decided I needed a shower. It had been a long morning. While in the shower, I kept thinking about Johnny and what he was told about his mother. I hoped he was safe and that Carlos would protect him. The thought of my little boy over in that horrible country made my skin crawl—I began to rub my protruding stomach over and over again. I promised my child that I would never let him or her out of my sight—not *ever!* I had two months to go before the delivery time. After my shower, I put fresh clothes on and decided to call my mother while waiting for Scott to come back. She always makes me feel good—I miss her.

Two hours later, Scott came through the door. He immediately came over to me, where I was sitting on the couch, and kissed me. I let him speak first.

"Well, the Captain believed what Fiona told him. To tell you the truth, Mac, I don't!"

"What? Why?" I said, surprised. "You can't really think that my sister would do anything that would hurt me!" I was getting furious. "Or Johnny, for that matter," I added.

"No, no, but there is something she isn't telling us—I can *feel* it!" He sat down on the couch in disgust. "Maybe, you can talk to her in private and coax her into telling you the truth. I don't know, tell her whatever she is hiding that you promise you won't get mad. Say that you to need to know everything she has done if you are ever to be close again." He looked at me, waiting for my response.

The problem was, I was feeling pretty uncomfortable at that point. Something was wrong. The contractions had started a few hours ago, which I had never mentioned to anyone. I had assumed it was those Braxton Hicks pains again—but I didn't think so this time! I turned to look at Scott, and he asked me what was wrong because I was white as a sheet. I grabbed onto the couch cushion and shook and moaned. I stood up and felt the wet drip down my leg—it was real!

"I think it's happening," I managed to get out of my mouth, which felt like I had swallowed cotton. Scott looked down at the floor and saw the puddle. Immediately, he ran into the kitchen, grabbed a towel, and we headed out the door to the hospital!

Chapter Twenty

I was able to hold my daughter for a few minutes, and then the nurses put her in an incubator and whisked her away. She was only three pounds, and she would stay in the incubator until she reached four pounds. The baby was seven weeks premature, and her lungs needed more time to get stronger, but the doctor assured us she was perfect in every other way. Scott held her briefly also. He was grinning from ear to ear—so proud of her. Now we had to think of a name.

"I suppose we should make some calls," Scott said to me.

"I'm going to call my mother," I said, "and you can call Frank and Fiona," I added. "Please ask them to call Elsie and Alison for me. How about Alice after my grandmother," I slipped in. Scott made a face.

"How many Alices do you know? It's kind of old fashioned," he said as he wrinkled up his nose.

"Well then, what name do you want?" I asked him.

"How about Molly?"

I smiled at him. "I like it. Molly, it will be if Alice can be the middle name!" I bargained.

"Molly Alice? Yikes! Okay, I'll agree to it." He then suggested, with a smile, we could call her Molly A—I agreed to do that. *At least on paper, she would be Molly Alice.*

It was very hard for me when it was time to go home, to leave Molly in the hospital. The doctor thought it wouldn't even be a month if she kept eating the way she was doing. I knew, though, I could go and be with her every day till she came home to us.

I hadn't been working for two years. The law firm was very understanding about my long leave because of all I had gone through these last few years. I wanted to discuss with Scott my going back to the Firm in the near future. I will tell him I miss it. I never attended the program at the college to become a lawyer like I had planned; I was content with being a paralegal for now. The lawyers were okay with my working part-time until Molly was a little older. My friend, Kelly, wanted to take care of my baby when I went back to work. The four of us had recently become good friends, and Kelly's husband, Mark, was in the service and was deployed now and again, which gave Kelly a lot of free time. They didn't have any children.

I had thought of everything so Scott wouldn't have an excuse to keep me at home. I needed to get back out there. Originally, Fiona was going to babysit if I decided to work nights when I had Johnny, but after finding out all the things she had kept from Scott and me, I don't want her to be alone with Molly for one second! It's taken me two years to get my life back on track, and I am determined to start living instead of grieving. Johnny is gone, and I know in my heart he is being protected from harm. I can only pray he will have a good life with Carlos and his family, but I will never understand why Carlos felt he needed to take my *pumpkin* away from me. At some point, I will talk to Scott about work and why he thinks Fiona is hiding something else—we have many things to discuss! *I might even bring up Anna!*

I stayed at the hospital overnight, for which I was glad. I was able to hold her in my arms, sing to her, and give her a bottle. I tried to breastfeed but wasn't able to do it. The nurse told me not to worry about it; sometimes, mothers can't, especially if they have gone through anything traumatic. She made me feel less of a failure. I loved when Scott had left to go home, and I was alone with her. She was truly beautiful. As I stared at her, I realized she reminded me so much of Johnny—same eyes and chin. My vision of Johnny was slowly disappearing, however, and I secretly hoped the pictures of him kept coming through the years.

Scott was relieved we had already prepared the bedroom for her arrival. We never expected it would be sooner than the due date. He told me he would make sure we had an adequate number of diapers, formula, and bottles on hand. I knew he was very reliable, and he would definitely be a hands-on dad. Before he left, he said he was going to stop by the station and brag about his daughter. We laughed, kissed, and then he left—p*eace and quiet at last.*

*I*n the morning, I called Scott and mentioned to him I was officially discharged but was going to visit till noon before I went home—I didn't want to leave her. The doctor was okay with me doing that because the more bonding we did, the easier it would be for her to adapt when she was released. Babies need to be close to their parents as much as possible in these situations. I would go home and then come back to give her the last feeding of the day. The nurses would give her the middle of the night feedings, which they told me was a good thing for us. We would be able to get proper sleep and be ready for anything when she came home.

*A*t around twelve-thirty, Scott arrived. He was disappointed he was not in time to feed her and wouldn't be able to in the evening either because he was doing the night shift all this week. That was okay by me; I was glad I would be going by myself tonight. We gave her our kisses, and I whispered to her I would be back at night and that her dad would see her in the morning. *Did she smile?*

*O*n the way home, we discussed all the things we still had to buy. I had felt bad because I hadn't been working and offered to take out some of my inheritance I received from my mother, but Scott insisted he could provide for us with no financial worries.

"That is so thoughtful of you; I will contribute once I start back to work." I waited for him to comment—he never did. He turned and smiled at me, and I quickly changed the subject. "What did they think at work when you told them about Molly?" I said, eager to find out. "Did you tell your mother and brother yet?" I also added.

"Slowdown, will you? You're rambling. Of course, everyone was excited for us, and my mother and brother were thrilled. After all, Molly is my mother's first grandchild, and my brother was thrilled that he was now an uncle. Also," he continued, "they will come to the hospital tomorrow to see her. I told them they could only peer through the glass because only you and I could hold her and be near her until her weight had climbed to a safe level. They didn't care; they just wanted to admire this new member of our family."

Chapter Twenty-One

Finally, we could take our Molly home. It had been three depressing weeks when I received a call one morning from the doctor to tell us Molly's weight was up to 4lbs, 2oz. I had to call Scott, who was on a daily schedule that week, to tell him the news. Unfortunately, he didn't answer his phone, which meant I would have to go by myself to pick her up. Before I left for the hospital, I tried again to call him—no answer. I then decided to call the station; maybe they could get hold of him. After a few minutes, they called me back and told me they couldn't reach him at the moment but left him an urgent message to meet me at the hospital—I was furious! I decided to call Kelly and see if she could go with me; luckily, she was available. *Where was he?*

I just wanted my life to get back to some semblance of normalcy. It seemed that Scott was taking every detail he could get. Did he not want to be home with me? I was hoping that once Molly was home, our marriage would get better—it would have a purpose. Kelly arrived, and she helped me put the car seat in the car, and off we went to the hospital.

When we arrived, I noticed Scott's patrol car outside in front of the entrance—number 57. When we went inside, Scott noticed us and quickly hurried up to me. He started immediately apologizing for not getting back to me. I glared at him.

"I thought that you told me I could reach you anytime at the number that you gave me." I was trying to control my anger because of where we were. "We can talk when we get home," I whispered to him. "Let's go get our daughter," I said out loud. Kelly, sensing the tension of our meeting, graciously told us she would wait down in the lobby.

Scott went into the car to retrieve the infant car seat while I went up to the second floor to the neonatal intensive care nursery to get Molly dressed to come home. Fiona had purchased a beautiful outfit for her to wear. I wasn't going to dress her in it because of how I was feeling about Fiona but decided I would, as she wanted a picture of this special day. I still had to talk with her about what she had done, making sure she had told us everything about what she knew had happened when we were at Disney World that day, so long ago—if anything.

I got excited when the nurse brought me my baby and placed her in my arms. She was making some gurgling sounds, which brought tears to my eyes. I changed her out of the little gown she had on and put on the dress from Fiona. Scott took a few pictures with our camera and then a few pictures of the nurses who took care of her. One of the nurses asked us if we wanted the three of us to have a picture taken together; we gladly handed her the camera. As soon as I could get out to the store, I would buy a special photo album for Molly.

On the way home, Kelly gushed over her and told us that she wanted to have a baby, but Mark did not think it was a good idea until he was out of the service. I mentioned that I could see his side of things—he was hardly home. She agreed with me but was still very frustrated over it. She explained how lonely she was when he was gone. I reached over and affectionately touched her arm. I couldn't imagine what she was going through and then reminded her that she would be part of our family because she would soon be babysitting for us in about a month. I decided I would get to know my baby before handing her over to someone else, as I wanted time to create a routine for her. I would only be working part-time to start—a few days a week.

When we pulled into the driveway, Scott's cruiser was already there. He came running out and opened up the back seat door to retrieve our daughter. As Kelly turned to tell us she was going home, Scott thanked her for being there for me. She hugged him and me and then grabbed Molly's little stubby fingers and kissed them. We said our goodbyes and went into the house—I was looking forward to being alone with Molly and Scott.

We took lots of pictures of her: undressing her, changing her diaper, Scott feeding Molly, Mom feeding Molly, and finally giving her a bath. Soon Molly fell asleep, and I quietly went upstairs and laid her in her crib. So far, she was a good baby; however, two hours later, she was screaming in her crib. We flew up the stairs to make sure she was all right; she needed to be changed and fed again. This went on through the whole night. *Ugh!* Thinking back, I didn't believe Johnny cried as much as Molly.

After the third night, we were exhausted. At least I didn't have to work in the morning as Scott did, but he never complained. It took us a few months to get her acclimated to some sort of routine—but we finally did it! Between all the company we had: his family and mine, and a few friends, we managed. I still hadn't said anything to Fiona, but that time was coming soon, however. After we finished sending out thank you cards and mailing pictures, we finally were able to relax and enjoy our little girl. She was now two months old!

I recently started back to work three days a week for six hours each. Kelly came over to the house on those days and took over for me. I left long lists for Kelly to follow, and I believed she was doing a great job. She never complained that things were difficult, even though I knew they had to have been—especially in the beginning. What would I ever do without her? And Scott was permanently put on days making things easier for everyone.

On one of the nights, Scott asked if I was ever going to talk to Fiona about what she knew about the kidnapping. I looked at him. *What?*

"I've been a little busy these past two months. I will definitely do it tomorrow on my day off." I didn't dare tell him I was uncertain about doing it. I didn't want to rip open old wounds.

"It's just that the office wants to fully rule out her involvement, and I had told them that I wasn't convinced she was telling the whole story. So, before they close her suspected involvement and move on, at my request, they wanted to wait till you spoke to her—if you were satisfied, they would be too.

"Okay then, tomorrow I will confront her." I turned and headed upstairs and said I was tired and was going to bed. He didn't follow me upstairs; things were not going well between us.

Chapter Twenty-Two

When I got up the next morning, Scott had already changed Molly and fed her before he went to work—he was good like that. However, I knew things were not the same with us. I called Kelly and hoped she could watch Molly for a few hours this morning. Otherwise, I would be forced to take her with me, which I didn't want because I didn't know how heated my conversation with Fiona would get. Luckily, she was free in the morning.

On my way over to see Fiona, I rehearsed all of the things I was going to discuss and all the questions I wanted to ask her. I made sure I brought both pictures of Johnny with me. Scott had made copies of the two pictures so I could have them; the police kept the originals. This visit was not going to be cordial! I had waited a long time to talk to her about any involvement she may or may not have had with Carlos. I felt this lie was not helping me with my relationship with my husband. Scott was very patient with me, even knowing I was constantly thinking of Carlos and Johnny, and I knew he must be ready to scream at me, as I have not been myself for months. *Why can't I just let them go and get on with my new life?*

I made the turn onto her street and pulled up in front of her house—Fiona would be the only one at home. I slowly got out of my car and looked around the yard—something was different! *Do I have the right house?* I walked around the side of the house and noticed the swings were gone, and then I glanced at the house itself and realized I was at the wrong house! How messed up am I?

One thing about Florida was that all the neighborhoods looked like. I chuckled to myself and thought, "No way was I going to tell anyone about this mishap, as they may put me away." I got into my car and drove two doors down to Fiona's place. There was her car parked right out front. If anything, this mistake lightened my mood a bit. I was very nervous as I got out of my car, and I had no idea what or how to begin my conversation about this very delicate subject. I knocked on the front door, and after a few minutes, she opened it.

"Hi!" she said, surprised, "I didn't expect to see you."

"Can I come in? We have to talk," I said as I pushed past her.

"Come right in," she gestured with her hand.

I walked right into the living room and sat down on the couch. She followed and sat in her recliner. I got right to the point. "Did you or did you not know that Carlos was planning to take Johnny to Cuba?" I could feel my face getting flushed, and immediately her eyes filled up with tears. "I don't want your tears, Fiona. I want the *truth!*" I was seething inside. "I mean it, do not lie to me!" I angrily added.

She put her head down on her hands and began to cry. "He, he," she began to stutter, and I could barely understand what she was mumbling to me.

"Fiona, stop it, stop the drama. You could always cry at the drop of a hat. You forget I lived with you. I watched you manipulate Mum and Dad. Even though I was just a little girl, I knew what you were doing. So, I'm not going to be sympathetic to your tears; please stop it this minute." I got up and walked over and stood in front of her. "I just don't want you to lie to me" She grabbed a tissue and wiped her eyes and nose. As she stood up to face me, I was sure she wanted to hug me; I stepped back a few steps waiting for her answer.

"It's complicated," she replied. "Mac, your dream was to come to America and go to college and someday become a successful lawyer." She reached out to grab my arms— I pulled back. "You were only *eighteen!* You were practically a baby yourself when you found out you were pregnant. There went all your hopes and dreams for a successful future."

"Says who? Was that something you decided? Sure, my plans would have had to change, but that was my decision. Do you hear me? *Mine.* When I first came here, I was jealous of what you had; I wanted that for myself. So, what did *you* do?" By that time, I was ready to slap her face. I could barely look at her as I felt the tears welling up in *my* eyes. What she told me next was shocking.

"After Carlos found out about the baby, he came to see me. He was happy but told me he wouldn't marry you, and he said you didn't want that anyway." She began to sniffle again.

I could feel my heart beating in my chest. I was petrified of what she would tell me next.

"Go on," I said, fighting back the tears. My tone had softened a little bit.

"Apparently, he had told you he wanted to take you and the baby to Cuba, but you told him you didn't want to go there. He told me he wanted his parents to see and hold their first grandchild—not just pictures."

I began to feel dizzy, so I sat back down on the couch. She also sat back down. "Why didn't you let me know that he reached out to you? All you kept telling me was that he was hiding something, and you didn't trust him." I was afraid of what she would say next.

"I was hoping you would say goodbye to him. Then I found out you moved in with him! After the baby was born, I was still suspicious of him, and I was afraid you would relent and go with him to Cuba, and I would never see you again. I then got in touch with him, and we had another meeting. I told him I knew he wanted you to permanently move there, so I might have suggested he just take Johnny to Cuba to visit. To *visit,* that is all! I had no idea he wouldn't come back. Honest, you have to believe me." She began crying again. "So, he then mentioned to me that you would never let him take Johnny to Cuba by himself. That is when I came up with the idea of taking you away for a couple of days while he took Johnny." She closed her eyes and hung her head.

I was shaking and crying all at the same time. I couldn't believe what she was saying. "Why didn't you tell the police this?" I managed to choke out.

"I could be arrested! What would I tell Don and the kids? I couldn't do that. Please, Mac, don't tell Scott. I don't want to go to jail. *Believe me;* I didn't think he would keep him."

I honestly didn't know what I would do, I stood up, looked at her, and spoke. "I know I never, *ever,* want to see you again! I don't know what I will do with this information, and I can't promise you anything. You're pathetic!" I turned and walked out the door.

On the way home, all I could think about was what to tell Scott and whether Fiona would get arrested if I told him everything. I didn't want that to happen, but what she did was *wrong!* I can't believe, in my heart, that she did this deliberately to hurt me. What should I do? I took the long way home to stall for more time. I saw a McDonald's and pulled into the lot—I needed time to think more clearly. I went through the drive-thru and ordered a coffee, as caffeine was what I needed. I found a parking spot further away from the building, pulled the car in, and turned off the ignition. I needed to go over everything that Fiona told me thus far before I went home—I had to make a decision. After about a half-hour, I knew *exactly* what I was going to do.

Chapter Twenty-Three

When I had left McDonald's to head for home, I was positive I was going to tell Scott everything Fiona confessed to me, but when I pulled into the driveway, I had changed my mind. I decided I wouldn't tell him anything because of what would be gained by getting Fiona arrested. I can't go back and do things differently; I would have to accept that Carlos and Johnny were gone from my life forever. When I turned into the driveway, I noticed Scott's patrol car. *Why was he home in the middle of the day? I hope Molly is okay!*

I screeched the car to a halt, jumped out, and quickly ran up the stairs. Before I opened the door, I took a deep breath. *Calm down, MacKenzie!* As I was about to turn the knob on the door, it opened, and Scott was standing there. He had a strained look on his face.

"Is Molly okay?" I was beside myself with fear.

"It's okay, Mac, everyone is fine. I need you to sit down because I have news regarding Carlos." He guided me into the living room and sat me down on the couch. My hands started to shake, and I was very frightened. He sat down beside me and held my hand. Kelly immediately left the room and went upstairs to check on Molly, who was napping.

"A body was discovered in the Keys in an area where they were bulldozing old houses to put up new condos." he paused for a minute to let me take in that information. "We aren't positive yet, but they think it was Carlos."

My body quickly went numb, and the tears seeped out of my eyes. Scott could see how upset I was and sensed immediately what I was thinking.

"No, Johnny was not with him. It was just one badly decomposed body. We found a wallet, a picture of a small boy, and a ring that he was wearing on his right hand. I am going to have to take you down to the station to see if you can identify any of those items. Are you calm enough to go with me now, or can we wait until tomorrow?" He put his arm around me.

My mind was muddled; there were so many questions going through my brain; I didn't know where to start. Is *Carlos dead?* My dream of Johnny and his dad living a wonderful life on his father's tobacco farm in Cuba was just destroyed. After I regained my composure, I told him that I wanted to go to the station now instead of tomorrow.

"Was he m-m-murdered?" I could barely get the words out.

"Yes, he was shot once in the back of the head. Pretty sure he died instantly, and we don't have any idea who or why."

"Okay, let me go upstairs to ask Kelly if she can stay longer, and I want to kiss Molly before we leave. I will only be a few minutes." I knew I was going to have to tell Scott about Carlos's illegal activities. I hoped I wouldn't be in trouble for keeping this to myself for all this time, and I needed them to know now because I wanted Carlos's killer or killers brought to justice. *Where is my son?*

On the way to the station, we barely spoke to each other. I was thinking of Carlos's smile and his white teeth. I could hear his laughter, and I remembered the day I told him I was pregnant and how mad he had been. I smiled to myself at the memory. When we drove into the parking lot, Scott turned and looked at me and reached for my hand.

"You're not going to have to see the remains, so don't worry," he squeezed my hand and continued. "Are you okay? It will be alright; I'm here."

I then got out of the car, and we walked with his arm around my shoulders into the building. Part of me was hoping it wouldn't be Carlos. Immediately, a woman came over and extended her hand to introduce herself to me.

"Hi, Mrs. Thomas. My name is Anna Wilson, Scott's partner," she smiled sweetly. "I wish I could have met you under different circumstances."

Anna? I looked at her beautiful long blond hair and striking blue eyes and then looked over at Scott as I shook my head slightly. I wasn't sure what I was feeling at that moment, but I knew that later on, we would have a talk! "Please, just bring the things over to me; I want to get home as soon as I can." I then looked right at Anna and told her I had to get back to my daughter.

"I understand; it will only be a second, Mrs. Thomas." She then left the room briefly to retrieve what they had found on his body.

I stared straight at Scott, and he knew immediately what I was thinking. In a couple of minutes, Anna appeared carrying a small container in a plastic bag. She had on gloves and told me not to touch anything with my hands—I could only look. As she began taking each item and placing them on the bag carefully, I immediately let out a gasp. I recognized Carlos's ring right away. I then looked at the picture of the small boy and knew it was Johnny. The wallet, though, I was not sure of, as it was empty. To me, it looked exactly like every other brown wallet I had ever seen. After I had identified the ring and picture, she quickly put everything back into the container. She thanked me for coming down to the station and for my help. I turned to Scott and quickly told him I wanted to leave. What was that glance Scott shot to Anna as she left to put the evidence back where she had taken it from?

On the way home, Scott tried to touch my hand, but I pulled it away. I was feeling very nauseous and asked him to please hurry, as I wasn't feeling very well. When we arrived home, I got out of the car and ran to the bathroom in the house, where I proceeded to vomit! When I came out, Scott and Kelly were discussing something, probably me. Molly was sitting in her little swing gnawing on her fist. She was teething, I assumed, and I went over and picked her up and held her tightly. I thanked Kelly for her help while slipping her some money. Although she tried to push it away and told me it was unnecessary, I made her take it. Finally, we were alone.

"I'm going to take a shower; it's been a long day. We can call for pizza instead of cooking if you like," Scott remarked as he headed for the stairs.

I guessed he wasn't in the mood for talking; I put Molly in her highchair with a couple of cheerios in front of her and went back to the bathroom. I began rummaging in the cabinet under the sink. I hadn't been feeling well for several days now, and I needed to find that *evil* stick!

Chapter Twenty-Four

Positive! How could this happen to me again? I continued to stare at the results. What would Scott have to say about this predicament! I threw the results into the rubbish and went back to where Molly was finishing her last bit of cheerios.

"Well, sweet baby, time for a bath and into your pj's." I picked Molly up and proceeded to the bathroom. This was Molly's favorite thing to do. She splashed and laughed, and I loved this time together with her. After her bath, I swooped her up and wrapped her in a towel, then took her upstairs to put on her pajamas. As I was headed into her room, I glanced in our room and saw Scott getting dressed. "Now, where are you going?" I sarcastically asked him.

"I have to go out for a short while. I know we have things to discuss, so I won't be long, I promise." He went over to Molly and gave her a kiss. I said nothing to him as he went down the stairs and out the door. I immediately went to the window and watched him drive away. After I fed and changed her diaper again, I put her to bed and then went into my bedroom, laid on the bed and began to cry—I was not happy!

I must have dozed off for a while because I heard someone rummaging around downstairs. "Scott must be home," I thought. I got up and looked at the clock; I had been asleep for two hours! I went into the bathroom and splashed some water on my face before I went downstairs to face the music. What I had to say to Scott was not going to go well—I was sure of that.

As I walked into the kitchen, he was washing a few dishes. "I brought home a salad and a pizza," he said as he turned to look at me. "You haven't eaten yet, have you? I was going to wake you, but you looked so comfy lying there. I already ate and saved you some."

"Thanks, I am hungry." I walked over to the refrigerator and took out the half pizza, and put it into the microwave to heat it up. After finishing eating my pizza and salad, I went into the living room where Scott was watching TV and walked directly towards the television to turn the volume down, then went over to the recliner and sat down. We stared at each other for a few minutes. I could see the wheels turning in his brain, wondering what was coming next.

"I'm pregnant again," I blurted out to him. His mouth dropped to the floor as he put his hands up in the air and stood up.

"Are you sure?" was all he asked.

"Well, I haven't seen a doctor; I just took a pregnancy test. I'm sorry; I don't know how this happened because I have been taking my birth control pills regularly.

"That was going to be my next question," he replied. "I am not going to pretend that I am happy about this; I guess it is something we will have to deal with."

"Have to *deal* with it?" I could feel my face getting red. I was so angry with him at this very moment. "Why didn't you tell me about Anna being your new partner?" The words flew out of my mouth. "Are you having an affair with her?" I didn't care how that sounded to him, but I suddenly felt relieved that what I had been thinking for weeks was now out in the open.

"*What*?" he retorted, "you're crazy," he finished. "I'm going up to bed!"

I followed him upstairs, "Why else would you not tell me your new partner was female? You have been taking on extra work and are hardly ever around. I have heard the two of you talking on the phone many times. You have never mentioned her once to me." I waited a few minutes, hoping he would just confess. Unfortunately, he never denied it or admitted to it. *Guilty!* "Answer me!" I screamed at him.

"Who *are* you?" he finally said, looking at me with contempt. "I will sleep in Molly's bedroom on the chaise lounge tonight. Think about what you are saying to me and maybe we can discuss it tomorrow when you come home from work. I am on the night shift tomorrow. Make an appointment to see your doctor. Goodnight!" He walked out of the bedroom and went into Molly's room.

"Good," I thought, "he will hear her if she wakes up for another bottle." Molly was four months old and still waking up during the night, probably because she is underweight. I quickly took a shower and went downstairs to watch some television before I went to bed. *Could I be mistaken?* After a couple of hours, I went upstairs, peeked into Molly's room, and saw her sleeping soundly in her crib with her butt up in the air—so cute. I glanced over towards the chaise and saw Scott snoring ever so softly. I smiled. *God, please let me be wrong.*

When I awoke, I dreaded going to work. Today was my day to work just six hours and Scott's turn to babysit. I got dressed, and as I was going downstairs, I checked on Molly. She was not in her crib. They must have gotten up early and were already downstairs. When I walked into the kitchen, Scott was feeding Molly, and he was singing to her. He turned and looked at me as I came into the kitchen. "She is all set for the day, so you can head right out to work, and we can discuss some things when you get home." Molly looked at me and started making all kinds of sounds.

"Sounds like she is trying to sing too." I chuckled. "Thanks for getting up with her, Scott." He grinned and then went into the other room. I ate my breakfast sitting beside Molly. "You're going to be a big sister, Moll." She *cooed* at my comment and then dropped her spoon on the floor. I picked it up and grabbed my things, gave Molly a kiss, and shouted to Scott that I was leaving so he wouldn't leave her alone in the highchair.

"Be right there," he yelled to me.

I tried to hold back my tears as I waved to Molly and walked out the back door.

Chapter Twenty-Five

Work was horrible; I wasn't concentrating because of all the questions I had going around in my head. What was I going to say to Scott, and what was he going to tell me? My boss approached me and asked what was wrong with me today. I briefly told him they had found the father of my missing son in a shallow grave but no sign of Johnny. He was so sorry and quickly told me to go home. I thanked him and said that is exactly what I wanted to do, and I mentioned to him that I would work eight hours on my next shift—he seemed pleased.

As I was headed home, I suddenly turned the car into someone's driveway and reversed my direction, and headed to the police station. I wondered if they had any more information about what had happened to Carlos. When I entered the building, I was hoping I wouldn't run into Anna, and then I realized she wouldn't be there because she would be working tonight with Scott. I was so infuriated with that thought. I checked in with the front desk and asked if there was a chance that I could talk to someone who had been working on Carlos Perez's case. She politely told me to wait a few minutes, and she would try and find out for me.

Within seconds a tall, older-looking police officer came around the corner and introduced himself to me.

"Hi there, Mrs. Thomas; my name is Lieutenant Bickford." He graciously extended his hand, and I quickly took it and told him it was nice to meet him. "I have taken over the case because of the relationships between Scott and some of the persons of interest in this case. Come into my office, and I will tell you what we think he was involved in and probably what had happened to him. Unfortunately, we know nothing about the whereabouts of your son—not yet anyway." I followed him into his office, where he instructed me to take a seat in the chair in front of his desk.

"I have something to share regarding what Carlos had told me after Johnny was born," I immediately volunteered as I sat down. The Lieutenant looked curiously at me.

"Do you think you should wait and call Scott first?" he said as he reached over to offer his phone.

"No," I emphatically stated. "I don't know why I had never mentioned it before to anyone, not even to Scott. Please tell me what *you* know, first."

He was a little hesitant, "I was going to reach out to you to show you some pictures of known drug dealers in the area that we think were connected to Carlos," he paused as he took a manila envelope from his desk drawer. "Since you are already here, would you be willing to look at these pictures to see if you recognize anyone you may have seen with Carlos at any time?"

Drug dealer? I was shocked as I heard those words come out of the Lieutenant's mouth. "Of course," I answered. I knew I should proceed cautiously, as I have learned a few things during the time I have worked in a lawyer's office. I carefully looked at each photo slowly, studying each face. There were five photos, and when I had gotten to the fourth picture, I stopped. In my head, I remembered the day I ran into Carlos at the coffee shop, just before our first date. This picture was of the friend that was behind Carlos as they were leaving. I would never forget his face because he had a visible scar right under his eye. I slid the picture towards the Lieutenant. "I have seen him at the coffee shop where Carlos and his friends used to hang out." I quickly asked him why he suspected drugs.

"They hung out there often?" he asked me. I nodded. He thanked me and then told me the gentlemen in the photos had been involved in drug smuggling for several years, but the department has never been able to acquire proof. "Each one of these men has been in this office many times. Regrettably, we have never had enough evidence to hold any of them. How Carlos died is a typical drug cartel shooting. Please write down the name of the coffee shop for me."

"Carlos never told me anything about drug smuggling. He did mention to me he was involved in smuggling people from his country, Cuba, to

America. He said all those people were hard up and needed to get out of Cuba. I knew it was illegal, but he made it sound like he was helping his people." I paused, "He promised he was done with all that because of Johnny. Sadly, I believed him." I handed him the name of the shop on a piece of paper and quickly began to whimper; my lips were cold and shivering. "Am I in trouble? I'm pregnant again."

The Lieutenant looked at me with a smile, patted my shoulder, and helped me stand up. "I want you to go home and tell Scott everything you have told me. Then at some point, I want you both to come back here, and I will pick your memory a little further. Don't worry, Mrs. Thomas; we want to find your son." I thanked him for being so kind to me.

When I got out of the car, I began to shake violently, and I knew I had to get control of myself before I went home. *Was Fiona involved in any of this?* I took a couple of deep breaths and then started the car and left the police station. Scott would be heading to work in a few hours, and I just wanted to get home, pick up Molly and squeeze her tightly. I loved her so much.

As soon as I walked through the door, Scott was on my case. He wanted to know what took me so long to get home and that he was very worried. I ignored his inquisition and asked him if Molly was napping. He informed me he had put her up for a little nap because she was very fussy after eating. I walked right past him and up the stairs to Molly's room.

"Mac, come back here. I want to know what took you so long. Where were you?" he shouted at the bottom of the steps.

"I have a headache; I want to kiss Molly, and I will be down later. We have a lot to talk about." I shouted down to him. When I walked into Molly's room, she was starting to whimper. I went over to her, picked her up, sat down on the rocking chair, and began to sing one of my silly songs to her—she smiled at me.

Chapter Twenty-Six

After about a half-hour, I brought Molly downstairs and put her in her playpen so I could talk to Scott; he was sitting on the couch watching TV.

"Let's go into the kitchen to talk just in case things get a little heated," I said as I started to walk out of the room.

Scott went over to Molly and kissed the top of her head, and handed her the teddy bear Fiona had given to her when she was born—it was her favorite. As Scott entered the kitchen, I immediately gave him a cup to hold for the coffee I started brewing.

"It will be ready in a few minutes," I told him

"Okay, where were you?" he asked as he sat down at the center island.

Without any hesitation, I blurted it out. "I went to the police station to try and find out if they knew anything more about Carlos's murder and confessed that I knew Carlos was smuggling people into this country illegally, and Lieutenant Bickford told me they suspected him for drug smuggling." I barely caught my breath.

"You confessed *what?*" His eyes widened.

"You heard me. I couldn't keep it inside any longer. Lieutenant Bickford asked if I wanted you there, but I told him no." I continued, "Evidently, Carlos had lied to me, and he was smuggling drugs, not people." I went over to the coffeemaker, took the flask, and poured some coffee for him and me. For a few minutes, neither of us spoke while we were busy stirring our coffee and cream.

He looked at me in amazement, then he spoke. "And then?"

I sipped my coffee as the teardrops rolled down my cheeks. Scott immediately put his cup down and came over to me. "I'm sorry I was so angry—I was worried. You should know you don't confess anything unless you have someone there to advise you. You work in a lawyer's office, for *Christ's sake.*" I was shocked because I had never heard him curse before. "What else happened there?" he asked.

I explained that the Lieutenant asked me to look at some photos, and I told him I had only recognized one picture and that he was a friend of Carlos's. "I also gave him the name of the coffee shop where he and his friends hung out most nights. The Lieutenant seemed very interested in that information, and he wants us to go back there so he can pick my brain a little more. Maybe they think I would have remembered something that they would deem important." I brushed the tears from my eyes.

"Have you made an appointment to see your gynecologist?" I think he desperately wanted to change the subject. I was determined to ask him if he was having an affair as soon as we were finished with my Carlos business. I knew he would probably fly off the handle when I did ask him.

"No, not yet; it's only been a few days since I took the test. I will go tomorrow after work." I promised.

He looked at his watch and realized he had to get ready for work. "I'm going to take a shower and change for work. We can finish our conversation tomorrow. I know you have something else on your mind, but I can't handle it right now. Please tend to Molly as she is crying a little." Then he left and went upstairs to shower, and I was relieved that my question would wait another day.

That evening, Kelly came over to visit and to find out if everything was all right between Scott and me. She explained that she thought there was something going on. *Should I tell her what I suspected?* The only thing I told her was that I was pretty sure I was pregnant again. Her reaction was surprising.

"Oh, my God! Was Scott happy about that?" She started to giggle a little bit and then apologized immediately. "I meant, he mentioned to me that he only wanted one child."

What? I was furious to think that Scott would talk about personal things to anyone, especially Kelly. I was going to respond to what she said but thought better of it. Instead, I said I was tired and that I had to get my clothes ready for work tomorrow. She quickly apologized again and said she would see me next week. I was glad Scott was going to be home all the rest of this week, during the day, to take care of Molly.

I went upstairs and pulled the things out of the closet that I would wear tomorrow and set them on the chair; I then checked in on Molly sleeping peacefully in her crib. She always makes me smile even when she is sleeping. Maybe tonight she will sleep through the night without waking for a bottle—and that is what she did.

Later on, I decided to call my mother because I hadn't talked to her in a couple of weeks. I had many things to share with her, and I hoped she wouldn't be very upset by anything I told her. I missed her very much and promised myself, once little *Rose* or *James* arrived, I would go back to England for a long visit with or without Scott; I needed to get away.

Chapter Twenty-Seven

The first thing I did before going to work was make an appointment with the gynecologist; that way, Scott would get off my back about it. I would be seeing her in a week, and I was almost positive I was pregnant—I had all the signs. Just as I hung up with the doctor's office, Scott came downstairs holding Molly.

"She is all changed, and I will feed her then give her a bath. Are you leaving now?" he asked as he put her in her highchair. "We will definitely talk when you come home this afternoon," he added.

"That will be good. I have an appointment with the doctor in a week; do you want to go?" I asked quietly as I walked over to Molly to give her a kiss goodbye.

"Of course, don't you want me to?"

I shrugged my shoulders and then said I had to leave. "See you around two," I replied.

What was happening to us? We were very polite and cordial. I hoped when I got home; we would be able to get things out into the open—his feelings and especially my feelings.

I could barely concentrate on my duties at work. My boss took me into his office and asked me what was going on with me. I had to tell him I was pregnant and had other personal problems. I felt I should give my notice because it wasn't fair to them for me to come to work and not give them my full attention. He was in agreement and held no animosity towards me. I informed him that I would finish out the day, or I would be willing to give him a week or two notice if that was what he needed. He said he would appreciate it if I could give him two weeks. I agreed willingly and thanked him for hiring me and being so understanding.

I left his office feeling relieved but couldn't understand why my life was turning into such a mess. I had to try harder to make my marriage work. *Another baby?* How was that going to help matters? I had to get the notion that Scott was having an affair out of my head. I truly hoped we could resolve all of this when I got home—unfortunately, it wasn't to be.

After I left the office, I stopped at the store and picked up a few items for dinner. I would make a really nice meal for us before Scott had to leave for work. When I rounded the corner that headed to our driveway, I noticed a police cruiser out in front of the condo. Scott's police car was at the station—whose was this? I parked my car, grabbed my grocery bag, and went quickly up the steps and into the house. I immediately heard voices; one was female!

I walked into the kitchen and saw Scott and *Anna* leaning over Molly laughing and joking with her. I startled them when I put the bag of groceries on the counter with a thud. Anna turned first.

"Mrs. Thomas, or may I call you MacKenzie? Your daughter is so beautiful; she is simply a delight." She smiled that sweet smile she gave me when we first met at the station.

I grinned. "Scott, isn't it a little early to be leaving for work?" I walked over to Molly and whipped her out of the highchair as I waited for an answer. He was in his uniform.

"I'm sorry, but I have to go in early. Anna came over to pick me up." He walked over and peeked into the bag to check out its contents. "Were you planning on cooking something special tonight?"

"Yup!" I was very curt with him as I began to put the things into the refrigerator with one hand and holding Molly on my hip with the other. I was deliberately ignoring Anna, and she knew it. "Will you be home all day tomorrow? I don't have to work, and weren't we going to discuss some things this afternoon?" He knew I was mad, but he didn't know *how* mad I was. He grabbed his hat and came over to give me a kiss. I turned my head and told him to have a safe night. Anna went out to the car, and as Scott left to follow, I told him I quit my job. The look of shock was all over his face. I then turned and took Molly upstairs. I decided to give her an early bath; then I would play with her and maybe read her a story—she would love that.

The evening crept up on me. It was time to feed Molly and put her to bed; we had a great time playing and reading her favorite book. It was so cute watching her try to change the pages quicker than I could finish the paragraph. She always made me feel relaxed and happy, but as I held her tightly, I started wondering about Johnny. *What happened to him?*

After putting her to bed, I took my shower and then got into my pajamas and went downstairs to call my mother. I felt like telling her my troubles, then thought better of it as she was a worrier; it's better that I keep things light. After our conversation, I fell asleep on the couch and was suddenly woken up by someone shaking me slightly.

"Mac," Scott whispered in my ear. "Let's go upstairs to bed; it's after midnight."

"Huh?" I was confused for a few seconds. "You're home already? What time is it?" I yawned.

"I left a little earlier because I started early, and I only had paperwork to catch up on. Do you want to talk now?" He grabbed my arms and pulled me off the couch. "Come on, let's go to bed. We will definitely talk tomorrow morning." I agreed and staggered up the stairs with him following behind me. That night he made love to me. *Maybe I am wrong!*

In the morning, over breakfast, he broached the subject of my job. I looked over at Molly, eating her cheerios all by herself. She was finally within the correct weight range for her age. Scott grabbed a jar of fruit and sat beside her, and started to feed her. She spent the time trying to grab the spoon till finally, he had to hold one arm down on the tray to put the spoon in her mouth. We both laughed at her.

"So, tell me about your job." he finally said to me.

"Well, I quit and gave them a two-week notice. I felt I wasn't able to concentrate, and I also mentioned that I was pregnant and would have to leave pretty soon anyway." I paused for a minute. "I also mentioned that I had some personal problems I was dealing with."

"Personal problems?" his eyebrows narrowed as he squinted, "Like what?"

I thought for a few minutes and then decided to just ask the question again. "Are you having an affair with Anna? You never gave me an answer before, and I deserve a *truthful* answer!" I tried not to raise my voice because I didn't want to scare Molly.

"*No!*" he answered quietly but firmly. "End of discussion!"

With that answer, he took the jar of applesauce and threw it in the rubbish, and walked out the door. I ran after him and screamed, "*I don't believe you!*" He jumped into the cruiser and took off down the street.

Chapter Twenty-Eight

My whole world was coming apart. I decided I would see if Fiona was home because I needed someone to talk to about all of this drama in my life—if she would even talk to me. Our lack of a relationship was tearing me apart inside. Could I forgive her? I wanted to in the worst way. She was my sister, and even though she made a terrible decision, I should try to forgive her. Thinking back and remembering the awful things I shouted at her, I wasn't sure she would even speak to me. I missed seeing her girls, and I knew she missed seeing Molly; in fact, she probably won't believe how big she had gotten. I walked over to the phone and picked it up, and began to dial...

Fiona told me to come over for a late lunch to talk, and that way, I would be able to see Margo and Maria when they came home from school. I agreed and told her I couldn't wait to see the girls. She asked if I could bring Molly because she missed her. I was going to ask Kelly to babysit for an hour or two but decided I wanted Molly to get to know her aunt. When I looked over at her, she was playing nicely with a toy in her playpen. I felt awful about telling her she had to take a little nap before going to see Aunt Fiona; hopefully, she will fall asleep fast—which she did.

When I arrived at the house, Fiona opened the door quickly, as if she had been waiting by the window, watching me, and I could tell immediately that she had been crying. She grabbed Molly from my arms and hugged her while tears trickled down her cheeks; my heart ached inside my chest. It had been three months since that awful day when Fiona confessed what she had schemed with Carlos. In order for me to move on, I needed to forgive her.

Fiona had made a very nice lunch of stuffed peppers, made with her famous taco stuffing, along with a small salad. I had brought along Molly's food, and Fiona delighted in feeding her while saying she couldn't believe the changes in Molly.

"How much does she weigh?" she asked while I handed Molly her bottle.

"About fifteen pounds. She has finally caught up to a normal weight gain for a five-month-old, and she is in the fiftieth percentile, which is average." I then added, "I think she is starting to try to say things; it is funny listening to her babble to herself before she falls asleep."

"I am so sorry for what I did to you." Suddenly, she threw her arms around me out of the blue. "Please forgive me; I love you."

"Fiona, I am trying very hard to forgive you, and I want you to know I feel really bad about saying those things to you, but I was in shock over everything that happened. My life was torn apart." I paused for a few minutes watching the two of them interact. She really was a good person. I then shocked her when I told her about Carlos being found murdered—she was speechless for a few minutes.

"Oh, I can't *believe* it! Do they know who did it and why? Do they know where Johnny is?" She closed her eyes and put her hands to her lips as if to pray. I had to stop the questions.

"All I can tell you is they are looking for some of his friends to question. I haven't heard anything more." I was starting to get choked up at the mention of my son, Johnny. I told her I didn't want to discuss it anymore for now and then blurted out that I was pretty sure I was pregnant again.

Fiona quickly came over to hug me, so I let her. It felt very nice to feel her arms around my body—it made me begin to blubber. When we both got our emotions under control, I began to tell her everything I suspected about Scott. She was in total disbelief and shock.

"Are you sure?" she asked when she had gotten over the shock of my statement. "I just can't believe he would do that to you."

I explained to her why I thought that and who I suspected was his *friend.* I told her I knew I hadn't been there for him like I should have been because I couldn't get Johnny or Carlos out of my brain, and I realized I had been monopolizing all my time with thoughts of where they were, but now that I knew what happened to Carlos, it is only natural that I would want to find my *son*!

"Fiona," I continued, "Why didn't he come to me and tell me he was confiding in Anna, and things were getting too close between them? I asked him point-blank if he was having an affair with her, and he denied it, but I can't shake the feeling I have."

"I have no easy answers for you, I'm afraid. I certainly think he should be more understanding about what you are going through and what you had gone through when he met you. He should understand that you would want to know the whereabouts of your son, and you're not going to just forget he ever existed!"

At that moment, the backdoor opened up, and two little cuties flew into the house. We never heard the bus pull up. Margo and Maria quickly ran over to me with arms flailing and screaming my name. Then they turned and noticed Molly in her playpen—the screaming continued. Molly was bouncing up and down on her bum; she was excited too. I knew at that time our discussion had come to an end for now. After about an hour of answering all kinds of questions about where I had been and all about Molly, it was time to pack things up and leave. Before I left, we made plans for all of us to go out to eat—all seven of us.

After we arrived home, I decided to take Molly for a little walk in her stroller around the complex, maybe go over to visit Kelly to see if she was home—killing some time before I would have to start dinner. I gave Molly a bottle with milk in it to tie her over till then. I had so much on my mind, but when I watched Molly holding the bottle all by herself, I smiled and felt happy.

Chapter Twenty-Nine

Today was the day Scott and I would be going to the doctor's office to corroborate my conclusion that I was truly pregnant again. On the drive over, Scott was suggesting different things that I might be experiencing and suggesting it probably wasn't a pregnancy. I guess he really was hoping it wasn't true.

"Boy, you really don't want another child, do you?" I was disgusted with his attitude.

"Look, it will only complicate things. We are going through a difficult time right now, and I don't think another baby will help matters!" He began twisting his hands back and forth while holding the steering wheel.

"Well, sorry. Somehow, I screwed up and forgot to take my pill. Believe me, I didn't do it on purpose, but I am sure I am right. I have peed on a stick three times, and each time it said *positive!* Feel free to leave if that is what you want to do. I'm sure it won't take you long to find someone else!"

"What does that mean?" he replied just as we pulled into the parking lot. He turned to me and suggested we get our act together in front of the doctor. I agreed.

Positive! The doctor seemed thrilled to tell us his findings. He was pretty sure I was almost four months. *What!* I had thought I was about two months along, so this was a true surprise. On our way out, I had to stop at the desk and set up all of my appointments and also an ultrasound—here we go again! All during the drive home, we barely spoke to one another. Scott broke the silence first.

"Do you want me to come with you tomorrow for the ultrasound?" He turned to look at me.

"You don't have to, it's in the morning, and you'll be at work." I let out a huge sigh.

"Why don't you ask Fiona to go with you since you made peace with her. I bet she will be tickled pink. If not, I will figure out something. Maybe Kelly could watch Molly for you?" His tone was soft.

"Yup, I will call my sister when I get home, and then we can ask Kelly if she is busy tomorrow morning to watch Molly for an hour or so again; I'm sure she will." Then I added, "I don't know what we would do without Kelly; she seems to be always available to babysit. Have you noticed she hardly ever talks about Mark anymore? Do you think they are still together?"

Scott hesitated before he spoke. "No, they aren't together anymore. She told me he reenlisted for another two years, so they are getting divorced."

"Really? She never said a word to me. That seems funny, doesn't it?" I looked over at him with some contempt. *Maybe I had the wrong friend!*

"Well," Scott said, "it could be because you are so wrapped up in finding out what happened to Johnny that she figured you had enough on your plate!"

I was just about ready to reply when he turned into our parking spot in front of the condo; I then shut my mouth. I will save my comments for after we eat and Molly is in bed. Molly was so excited to see us, and after a few minutes telling Kelly what the doctor had told us, Scott paid her. As she was about to leave, I went to Kelly to say I was sorry that Mark and she were splitting up. Kelly thanked me and gave me a hug, and said we could talk about it another time.

Scott immediately pounced. "Why did you bring that up? Maybe she didn't want anyone to know yet; she told me in confidence."

"I bet she did!" I replied sarcastically. "Can we talk later? I want to go for a walk with Molly; she and I need some fresh air." I went to the closet, dragged out her stroller, put her in it, and started for the door. Scott gave me the evil eye and went into the other room. "Ahh," I said, sniffing the air once I was outside. "Isn't this fun, Molly?"

Molly giggled and gurgled as we started down the driveway. I began to talk to her like she was an adult, telling her all about my feelings and about her new baby sister or brother she would have in a few months. She was busy jiggling her pretend keys and putting them into her mouth. I loved this stroller because she was facing me instead of away from me, and we could really have a conversation; I laughed at that thought as we began to walk on the sidewalk.

After about a half-hour, I realized I had walked to the coffee house that Carlos and I had gone to many times. I decided I would bring Molly in and get a couple of muffins to bring home for Scott and me—a peace offering from his *bitchy* wife. It wasn't too crowded, of which I was glad because it was hard to maneuver the stroller between the tables. Just as I reached the counter, someone stepped in front of the stroller. I was just about to excuse myself when I recognized that scar under his eye. I gasped as bile came up into my throat.

"Hi, there!" he mumbled, "remember me?" His look was menacing.

I had to think quickly, "No, should I?" He glared at me. "Excuse me; you're keeping me from the counter." I was proud of myself how quickly I regained my composure.

"Sorry, I thought I recognized you as someone I had met a long time ago." He moved to the side and waved me on, then he and three others quickly left the premises.

I immediately leaned over and kissed Molly. The gentleman at the counter asked me if they had bothered me; I told the clerk that everything was fine, and the man had thought he knew me, that was all. I ordered my two muffins and then quickly exited the coffee shop, all the while checking to make sure they were gone. I would call Lieutenant Bickford when I got home.

Chapter Thirty

I practically ran all the way home with Molly laughing as we went, and I was completely winded by the time I got into the house. I grabbed Molly out of the stroller and went urgently into the living room where Scott was watching television. I quickly passed her to him and started to dial the police station. Scott immediately got up and put his finger on the hang-up button.

"*What* is the matter? You look like you have seen a ghost! Now, come over here and sit down and tell me what's the matter." He placed Molly in her playpen and handed her a toy.

I began to tell him what had transpired at the coffee shop and that I needed to call Lieutenant Bickford right away to let him know I saw and briefly spoke to the man in the photo with the scar under his eye. I knew I was rambling, and I watched as Scott tried to figure out what I was talking about. I was still breathing heavily and had started trembling.

"Please, slow down, Mac." He came and sat beside me and placed his hand over mine to try to help stop the shaking. "Let's start over and tell me what happened from the beginning."

After I had calmed down, I began to tell him everything. He wanted to know if I had felt threatened in any way, and did I think he would have harmed me. I told him I had just panicked for a moment because he had caught me by surprise and really didn't feel in any danger—there were too many people around. I said I had made sure I wasn't being followed and was fairly certain he believed me when I said I didn't know him.

When I was done telling my tale, he walked over to the phone and dialed the station. I went over to the playpen and began playing with Molly. After a few minutes, he sat down and handed me the phone and said the Lieutenant wanted to hear it directly from me. I took the phone and went out to the kitchen and began my story again. The Lieutenant mentioned that he and a few officers had gone to the shop a few weeks prior, but no one remembered seeing any of the men in the photos. Before he hung up, he said they were going to head over to the shop now and maybe would get lucky with the gentleman who was working behind the counter; he would certainly remember the recent confrontation.

When I had mentioned to Scott what the Lieutenant was going to do, he quickly told me he wanted to be there and did I mind if he went. Of course, I said I didn't have a problem with it. In fact, I said I would feel much better if he could hear what the owner had to say about everything. I knew all of those same guys went to that coffee house frequently— someone is lying. *They have to know where Johnny is!*

While Scott was out, I changed, fed, and bathed Molly. When I had put Molly back in her playpen because it was still a little too early for bed, I called Fiona to see if she could go with me tomorrow for my ultrasound— she was excited that I had asked her. I then decided to call my mother and give her an update as to what was happening—that was a big mistake!

"What?" my mother sounded frightened. "You need to take Molly and come home to us immediately, please, MacKenzie. I will talk to Scott about it when you aren't around."

"Mum, I am not in danger; I am positive he believed me. I pushed the panic button briefly; that was all. If you are going to react this way, I won't confide in you anymore. If I thought for one moment I was in danger, I wouldn't stay here, and I know Scott would whisk me away somewhere, so please don't worry, promise me?" *Was I in danger?*

I had quickly changed the subject and talked about the visit to the doctor and told her I had been right and I was pregnant—four months. She was so happy for me. The only thing I didn't tell her about was how Scott and I hadn't been getting along lately; I felt she didn't need to hear that on top of everything else. She babbled on about my sisters and brother and all their accomplishments. I glanced at the clock and realized it had been almost two hours since Scott left; I hoped everything was okay. I ended my call to my mother quickly when I finally heard Scott entering the house through the kitchen door, followed by—*Kelly!*

I picked up Molly and yelled to Scott I was going upstairs to change Molly and would he get her bottle ready. I certainly couldn't understand why Kelly came over, and I wasn't going to discuss anything about what had happened earlier with *her*. After about ten minutes, I went downstairs, and there she was, smiling as always. *GRRR.* I handed Molly to Scott and asked him to give her the bottle; then, I went over to Kelly and politely asked her if she would mind leaving because Scott and I had personal things to discuss. At first, she didn't understand my request; then, she caught on.

"Oh, I'm sorry, of course, I will. I will talk to you later."

It seemed to me she was over here a lot. I think I will ease up asking her to sit with Molly and let Fiona do that if I need someone. Fiona only worked three days a week, so I would make my doctor appointments on her days off and use Kelly for emergency purposes only. Scott may not agree, but that is what I want!

When she had left, I went into the living room and saw Molly lying in Scott's arms sucking away at her bottle; they looked so cute together. She was growing so fast that you would never have suspected she spent a few weeks in an incubator because of the early birth. I sat down beside Scott, and we began to play with Molly's piggies, which we both loved to do. She started giggling and choking a little on the milk she was drinking. We quickly sat her up and heard the huge burp come out of her—we both looked at each other and laughed out loud. These times were so peaceful and comforting to us both.

I posed the question first, "What did you find out?"

He put Molly on a blanket on the floor and watched as she got up on all fours. Yes, she would be crawling before long. He then started from the beginning.

"Luckily, when we arrived there, the gentleman behind the counter was the manager, and he remembered you immediately. The problem before was that the manager wasn't there to talk to the police, and the girl behind the counter on that day had never seen the men in the pictures before. The manager looked at the pictures and told us all five of them, including Carlos, frequented the coffee shop at least once a week, but he noted Carlos hadn't been there in months." He paused a few minutes to play with Molly. "He was very co-operative and told Lieutenant Bickford he would call him when they came in again."

"Well, that's something anyway, I guess." I went into the kitchen to start our dinner, followed by Scott. He added that the manager said they never caused any trouble when they were in his shop.

I looked at Scott and just said what was on my mind. "Are you having an affair with Kelly?"

"Here we go again! *NO, NO*, and *NO!* That is the last of the accusations. What is wrong with you? I want you to go see someone. I'm not going to continue to defend myself to you. We are having another *baby,* for crying out loud! If you want out, there's the door." he said, pointing to the door. "I'm going to get ready for work, don't wait up for me."

With that comment, he went upstairs. I was glad that I got it out of my system. I then went to the foot of the stairs, and with tears in my eyes, I told him my mother wanted me to visit, and maybe I would take Molly for her first plane ride—he didn't answer.

Chapter Thirty-One

A few weeks had gone by since our last serious argument. We were being polite to one another, talking only when we had to. It was a nightmare! I was still thinking about taking a trip to England to see my mother, Eileen, Daniel, and Bonnie. Bonnie had gotten married since I had left home three years ago. She was now pregnant with her first child. I checked with the doctor; he had advised against traveling that far because of my history of having Molly almost two months early. I guess I will have to wait till after the baby is born. I had almost four months to go.

We hadn't heard anything from Lieutenant Bickford regarding Carlos's friends going to the coffee shop. I had wondered if I had scared them off, and he thought I *did* recognize him. I was anxious, wasn't sleeping well. Perhaps I *should* go see someone professionally again. I think of Johnny every day, but I dare not mention it to anyone. This whole thing is consuming me. Fiona checked in on me regularly, and Kelly still popped in unannounced, always right after Scott left for work. I was polite to her, but she kept going on about how upset Scott was and how depressed I seemed. I think she was trying to help and to keep me occupied. She told me Scott was so worried. *Well, who has she been talking to?*

On this particular day, no one came over or called me, and I was feeling pretty depressed. Molly had a little cold, and I didn't dare take her outside anywhere. I decided I would clean out one of my upper kitchen cabinets; it served no purpose other than throwing things up there that didn't have a specific place. I dragged the step stool out from the back closet after I had put Molly down for a nap. The poor thing had a stuffy nose, so I made up a bunch of blankets on the rug in the living room. I surrounded her with pillows, and she went out like a light.

I was on my tippy toes on the top step of the stool, trying to get some hard-to-reach things, when my doorbell rang. It surprised me because I wasn't expecting anyone. *Damn.* I carefully held on and climbed down the three steps. I wiped my hands on a dishtowel I had hanging over my shoulder and peeked in on Molly—she was sleeping soundly. I secretly hoped it wasn't Kelly because I might not be hospitable. I looked out of the window and couldn't see anyone, so I decided to open the door. There sitting on the porch was a suitcase—it was familiar to me.

"Where have I seen that before?" I said to no one in particular. I bent down to bring it into the house, all the while looking all around the front of the house. I didn't remember ever asking to use someone's suitcase because I wasn't going to England like I had wanted to. I didn't believe it was Scott's. When I picked it up, it was not light by any means—something was inside.

I brought it into the kitchen and put it on the floor. I didn't want to lift it up onto the table because it was heavy, and the doctor frowned on lifting things that were too heavy. I somehow managed to get down on my knees in front of the suitcase. It was getting harder for me to get up and down or bend over. This was definitely the last time I would be pregnant. I had already decided I would get my tubes tied after the baby was born—this was not happening again. I tried to open it up, but it seemed to be locked. There was no key; I guess I will have to pick the lock. Oh boy! I have always wanted to pick a lock just to see if I could figure it out. I struggled to get up off the floor and head to a junk drawer that had a few tools thrown in among pencils, tape measures, odd spoons, and old receipts, etc. After rummaging through a lot of useless things, I found a small pick. This may do it.

I stopped and peeked in on Molly; she had shifted herself but was still asleep. "Good," I thought to myself, "she needs her sleep." I knelt on the floor again; I felt like I was a hundred years old because of the noises I made. I stroked my stomach and was amazed at how active this child was being. Once I got into a comfy position, I began to pick at it. It took a few minutes before I heard it click. Finally, it was unlocked.

I slowly started to lift the cover-up; I was feeling a little uneasy and didn't know why. When the cover was fully open, I was in total shock at what I was seeing. I immediately started to pick the clothes up and look at them. There before me were all of Johnny's baby clothes. I continued to rummage through and found books and something that looked like a journal. At the bottom was a scrapbook filled with pictures of Johnny, Carlos, and what I had assumed was Carlos's mother. Underneath everything was Johnny's little bear that Fiona had given him after he was born. I practically collapsed on the floor. I flopped on top of his clothes, and one by one, picked up each piece, the memories flooding my mind. I smelled each one and truly thought I could still smell him. I began to cry uncontrollably; I knew I should call someone, so I decided to call the station and get a hold of Scott. Molly would be waking soon, and I didn't think I could handle her.

I rambled on to the dispatcher and told her who I was and that I needed Scott right away. She asked me if I needed an ambulance, and I told her no, just send Scott home! Within minutes Scott's cruiser pulled up along with an ambulance. He flew into the house and saw me on the floor hanging over a suitcase. The EMT driver came in with him; I pointed to Molly because she had begun to cry.

"My God, Mac, what is the matter? Is Molly okay?" I was too hysterical to speak. He picked me up and brought me to the couch, then noticed the suitcase. "Who gave you that?" He realized it was baby clothes. Then, he started looking through all of the things and eventually put together what had happened.

"The they are Johnny's things," I managed to get out. I then flopped over on the couch.

Chapter Thirty-Two

I didn't wake up till the next morning. *What did they give me?* I do remember having some sort of shot in my arm. *Was I that bad?* I managed to get out of bed and make it to the shower; I felt great relief feeling the water pour down over my weary body. I scrubbed myself like I was trying to get rid of all the heartache I went through the day before. Slowly, I felt myself sliding down the shower wall, and there I remained until Scott came upstairs looking for me. The water was still spraying all over me as I sat there and whimpered.

"Mac," Scott called for me. He heard the water running and quickly went into the bathroom and pulled the curtain open to find me in an uncompromising position. "Oh, Mac," he asked me in a sympathetic way. "Are you okay?" He lifted me up, shut the water off, wrapped me in a towel, and brought me back to the bed.

"Is Molly alright?" was the first thing out of my mouth. "I'm so sorry, Scott. I guess I lost it, huh?"

"We are going to get you dressed because I made an appointment today with the therapist you had before. Everyone agrees, along with your therapist, that you need to be seen right away."

I knew he was right, so I didn't try to fight him about it. I dressed willingly and followed him downstairs to have something to eat and hold Molly. As we were eating, Scott explained everything that had happened when he arrived home yesterday. He said the police took the suitcase and its contents to see if there were any fingerprints that may point to the person who dropped off the suitcase. *Suitcase*—that word stung! I insisted we take

Molly with us; I wasn't leaving her with anyone. Scott agreed, and he said he would take the stroller with us, and while I was in seeing the doctor, he would take a walk outside with Molly.

When I was through with my appointment, I went outside and looked for both of them. After a couple of minutes, I noticed they were sitting outside the ice cream shop across the street; Molly was holding the broken end of Scott's ice cream cone with just a small amount of vanilla ice cream on top—a miniature cone. I grinned as I crossed the street to try to surprise them, but Scott glanced up and saw me approaching; he was smiling.

"Sorry she is a mess, but look how much she is enjoying this," he said, feeling proud of himself.

"That's okay; she will clean up real nice when we get home," I replied as I tried to wipe some of the ice cream from her face with the sleeve of my blouse.

On the way home, Scott stopped and bought some Chinese food to take home. He knew I was drained emotionally and mentioned he wasn't working tonight and would take complete charge of Molly so I could rest. I knew he was nervous because of my behavior yesterday.

"I am going to be okay, Scott." I reached over and touched his leg as he drove. "My session with the doctor helped me a lot," I assured him.

Soon we were home, and he brought Molly upstairs, cleaned her up, and then brought her back downstairs to prepare her meal. I told him I wanted to help her feed herself; I would rest after we had *our* Chinese food—he understood. Molly played while we ate our dinner. A calming feeling came over me as I watched her play with her toys. "*Aah*, to be so sweet and innocent," I thought. "She really was a well-behaved baby, so lucky to have her," I thought to myself, "and soon there would be another one in a few months." I knew at that moment I had to get it together before the baby was born; I've got to forget about the past and concentrate on my future—for my children's sake. That was one of the things my therapist tried to instill in me when we talked, but she just didn't get it. How can anyone forget they had a child who disappeared without a trace?

"What are you thinking about, Mackenzie?" Scott said, interrupting my thoughts.

I looked at him and smiled. "I was just thinking how difficult it will be with two toddlers running around." I lied.

"We will manage, so don't worry about it," he replied as he got up to clear away the dishes for me. "Why don't you go into the living room and watch some TV? I will tend to the dishes and take care of Molly," he added.

"Thank you. She is really very good, isn't she?" I asked him. He looked at her and then at me while nodding.

I wanted very much to sit down and talk to Scott about the suitcase. I wanted his take on it and if he had any ideas about who could have left it. I knew better, though, best keep those thoughts to myself for now. When he goes back to work, I will discuss it with Fiona—see what she thought. While watching television, I heard a knock on the kitchen door; the hairs stood up on the back of my neck, which made me shiver—I then heard Kelly's voice. *Go away!*

I wasn't going to get up; I just turned the TV down a bit so I could hear what they were saying about the *crazy wife!* I knew Scott was probably telling her I was in the living room watching TV. I was hoping she wouldn't come in to say hello—but she did!

"Hi, Mac, how are you feeling today? How did your visit with your therapist go?" Kelly said to me as she walked into the living room.

I heard Scott in the kitchen. "Kelly!" he sternly shouted to her.

"It's okay, Scott. I don't mind," I yelled to him. *What nerve!* "Kelly, I am fine, don't worry about me," I answered sweetly without really looking at her. I suppose she means well, but I still have my suspicions, and I will keep them to myself.

Chapter Thirty-Three

During the next three months while waiting for our second child to be born, Scott and I became more *friends* than a husband and wife. I think we both realized that we jumped into this marriage because of Molly and were thrown together through my tragedy. I was only nineteen when it all happened, and Scott was twenty-six. We sat down and had a serious talk about what to do while promising that he would be here for me and stay with me for as long as I wanted him; he would be a wonderful father to our daughter and the new baby when he or she arrived in a few weeks. Sometimes, deep inside, I wished I had fallen in love with him completely, but he was more like a good friend or even a brother except for the sex, of course. So, we had an arrangement of sorts and never told anyone else about it—at least I didn't.

We did hear that the gentleman with the scar under his eye was Carlos's best friend. The detectives finally had gathered enough evidence against Jose to arrest him for drug smuggling but couldn't pin Carlos's murder on him or any of the others in their group. Lieutenant Bickford told Scott that they thought Carlos's murder was probably done by someone higher up in the drug chain. Jose confessed to delivering the suitcase to me per orders from Carlos in case something happened to him. I was given the journal from the suitcase, which had been written in Carlos's handwriting. It never mentioned where Johnny was but did depict his day-to-day activities up until Carlos disappeared. This journal was very cathartic for me because I knew, in my heart, Johnny was out there somewhere with someone who loved him. I felt I could now move on with my life and raise and treasure my children.

One day, as I was out walking Molly, I felt a jabbing pain in my lower abdomen. I still had a few weeks before I was due to give birth, but because Molly had come early, it could be time. What was I going to do? I was not near any stores or condos. Each time I began to walk, the pain started again, then my water broke on the sidewalk, and I was doubled over. I looked around and decided I had to cross the street and knock on the first door I came to because the baby would be coming quickly. I have no idea how I managed to get across the street pushing the stroller, but I made it and banged on the first door I saw. A woman came to the door and took one look at me, and called the police. I will be eternally grateful for her kindness.

The next thing I knew, I was looking at Scott's face as he held our daughter in his arms; what a great man he was. We named her Rose after my mother. Tomorrow, I will go back into surgery and have my Tubal Ligation. The doctors tried to talk me out of going through with it because I was only twenty-two, but I was adamant about never having another child. By the time I came home, I was pretty sore. Fiona, Scott, *and Kelly* were very helpful by fussing over me and helping with the care of Molly and Rose. After a couple of weeks, things were much easier because I felt much better. Taking care of a ten-month-old and an almost one-month-old was going to be challenging, to say the least!

As the months passed swiftly by, I never found out anything more about Johnny's whereabouts or who exactly helped Carlos disappear and who caused his death. I was kept busy with my children and trying to make this platonic relationship work between Scott and me without telling everyone about our arrangement. I knew, in my heart, that the agreement Scott and I had between us was not going to last forever because I still had my suspicions about Kelly, but I didn't blame Scott for the cheating if that was what was going on. I never mentioned anything more about his being unfaithful because what was the point; I didn't want any arguments to ensue.

When the girls were three and two, I asked Scott if he minded if I went to England for a couple of weeks, as I hadn't visited my mother for a few years and wanted her to meet her grandchildren in person. He had asked me if I wanted him to come along, but I had told him I really wanted to do this with just the three of us. He didn't know that I wanted to tell my mother everything that had been going on—she had a right to know. I had been saving some money these last few years because I knew I would eventually leave Scott for good before the girls entered school. I wanted to move out of Florida and get away from all the heartache and nightmares and decided to head north to New England. I wanted to purchase a home with the remaining money I had left from my inheritance and get back into the workforce. I would move somewhere near Elsie and Alison and hopefully, renew our kinship and be close with one another again.

Soon the day arrived that Molly, Rose, and I were going to head to England. The girls were so excited about going on a huge plane and flying to see their grandmother. I explained everything that would happen when we were in the air and that they probably would be napping the whole way; I was very excited also. Molly was thrilled about meeting *Grandmother,* as well as Aunt Eileen, Aunt Bonnie, and Uncle Danny. They were, of course, just as excited to see all of us; it would be a joyous and fun reunion!

When we landed, I had to wake up both girls because they had slept most of the way, and even though they missed a lot, they acted as though they had been awake the whole time. My family met us at the airport, and I couldn't believe how Molly and Rose took to everyone, as they were basically shy with new people. Of course, they had spoken to their aunts and uncle many times on the phone, but this was a much better situation for them, as you could imagine. For the sake of the girls, I had to fight back my tears at the sight of them all lined up waiting for us to get off of the plane—it was great to be back in England!

The two weeks we spent with my family were not nearly enough time. In a blink of an eye, it was over, and then it was time to leave. Unfortunately, once we arrived back home, I found that my misery and suffering surfaced once again!

Chapter Thirty-Four

We had been home about a week when I received frightening news from Lieutenant Bickford. Scott had been spending a lot of time with Rose and Molly because he had taken a couple of weeks off from work—he had missed them very much. Fortunately, Rose and Molly were visiting with Kelly, and Scott and I had been home alone when I got the call.

I picked up the phone and said hello, and recognized the Lieutenant's voice. Immediately, I had a terrible feeling in the pit of my stomach. Scott entered the room, and I handed him the receiver; I didn't want to hear what the Lieutenant had to say.

"Scott, this is Lieutenant Bickford; I was wondering if you and MacKenzie could come down to the station now because I have something to discuss with you both, and I don't feel it is the type of thing to relay over the phone. If it is better for you both, I could come to the house."

Scott looked over at me and then replied to the Lieutenant that we would be there in a short while. He then contacted Kelly and asked her if she could keep the girls a while longer, which of course, she said she would. My heart was beating out of my chest. *Will my nightmare never end?* Scott came over to me and held me while explaining what was said on the phone.

"Mac, don't go imagining the worst. Maybe it has to do with Carlos, so let's not over-think what the Lieutenant told me; that's how he does things." I nodded as I began to shake.

On the drive over, I never said a word. I stared out the car window and watched as the trees, condos, and stores went by. We passed the coffee shop where Carlos had taken me on our first date. I was trying to remember the first song he played on the jukebox that was by the booth we sat in—but I couldn't think. In about twenty minutes we arrived at the police station. Scott looked at me with pity in his eyes. There were no tears falling down my cheeks as I looked over at him, and I think he was a little worried about what was going to be said in a few minutes and how to handle *me* if it was bad news. I walked like a Zombie—my eyes facing straight ahead— into the station while holding onto Scott's hand.

Immediately, the Lieutenant came over to greet us and directed us into a small room while shutting the door behind him. *Here it comes!* He motioned for us to have a seat, shuffled some papers around, and began speaking softly, staring right at me. I only heard the words: boy, woods, dead. Everything else was a blur.

"Have you identified him?" Scott said, grabbing my hand tightly.

"No, we found a comb in Johnny's suitcase; it had a piece of hair attached, and we took a piece of the deceased's hair and sent them both out for DNA testing. I can't promise if this will absolutely identify the body as being little Johnny because DNA testing is fairly new, but I am hopeful." he looked over at me with sympathy. "I'm sorry, Mrs. Thomas," he added.

Scott quickly spoke up, "It could also prove that it *wasn't* Johnny, right?"

"Of course, absolutely. The boy was around two to two and a half years old. He had on a red striped jersey and blue pants. That is all we have to go on. We checked and found out there had been only three small boys who had gone missing in the last few years around this area."

"When will you know?" I asked calmly. I still had a blank look in my eyes.

At those words, Scott looked at me, surprised at my calmness. The Lieutenant told us it would take about seventy-two hours to receive the results, and he would call us as soon as he found out anything. We then thanked him and left. I walked quickly out to the car when Scott spoke first as we were getting inside the vehicle.

"Mac, are you okay?" he asked cautiously.

"Absolutely, I am positive that little boy is not Johnny. Johnny is living with someone who loves him and will take care of him. I have a strong feeling about that!"

His look gave me the shivers. He was waiting for me to break down, but I wasn't going to because I truly believed it wasn't Johnny. Scott had asked me if I wanted to tell my therapist today about what had happened instead of waiting till next week at my appointment. I told him no; we might as well wait till we hear the results.

"Are you sure you want to wait?" He was skeptical.

I nodded, and when we arrived home, I mentioned to him I was going upstairs to lie down and asked if he would get the girls and bring them home to me as soon as possible—I needed some hugs!

The next three days were the worst days of my life. Waiting for an answer from the tests was killing me inside, but I wasn't going to let my true feelings about all this be known to anyone. I had called Frank and Fiona to let them know what had transpired. Fiona wanted to come over right away, but I explained I really just needed to be alone with Scott and the girls during this waiting period. I told her I really appreciated her concern, and I would let them both know as soon as we knew.

On the third day, while eating our breakfast, we received *the* phone call. It had been a hectic morning because the girls were stubborn about everything. It seemed that when Molly did something or touched something she wasn't supposed to, Rose would imitate her. *Double trouble!* When I heard the phone ring, I wanted to run away. Scott answered the call.

I quickly grabbed the girls and went upstairs; I didn't want to hear the answer. While upstairs, I got Rose and Molly dressed for the day. Molly was so smart, as she was already potty trained, but Rose, on the other hand, was having no part of that toilet seat!

I decided to go back downstairs and settle the girls in the living room on their favorite tiny rocking chairs and start them watching their favorite cartoon show. I could hear a little bit of what Scott was saying to his boss but not clearly. I knew I would have about a half-hour before the girls would get restless and begin looking for me. I quickly hurried into the kitchen just as he hung up the phone, and when he saw me, he smiled.

"Not a match! It wasn't him!" he waited for me to collapse.

I immediately began to cry as I ran into his arms. "I knew it! I knew it!" I yelled out loud. I was never happier, and Johnny was safe and living with someone who loved him. I felt awful for the parents of the missing child, as they must be going through hell like I am. My hope being that the child's family can be located someday, and he can be laid to rest.

Chapter Thirty-Five

Later in the evening of that day, when Scott and I had put the kids to bed for the night, he dragged me into the living room to have a heart-to-heart talk. I was happy and didn't want to discuss anything about my missing son anymore. He told me I was living in a dream world, and I refused to accept reality.

"I know you want to believe in a fairy tale ending to the hell you have gone through, but you must realize the possibility of anyone finding Johnny is practically non-existent. Mac, it has been five years! I am hoping that you will eventually have closure to all of this, but you need to be, at least, aware that it may not end as you wish; that's all I am saying to you. *You* have to face the reality of the situation," he lectured.

I just stared at him, and at that moment, I knew I would begin my plans to leave him within the next year. Molly would be four and Rose three. I would keep everything to myself for a while because I still hadn't saved as much as I had wanted, but I didn't want to be around anyone who was negative anymore. I took a job at a nearby department store for two days a week. Scott thought that would be a great idea for the health of my mind. Fiona said she would sit with the girls on one of the days and Kelly (I hated to ask her) agreed to the other day—that problem solved.

One day, when several months had passed, I was taking a walk alone to help clear my head. I was thinking about when was the right time to leave everything behind and whether to tell Scott beforehand or just leave. I realized, legally, I couldn't just leave with our children without Scott's consent. I hated the thought of confronting him even though he knew eventually we would be separating; it was best for him and also me. The kids would definitely miss their dad, especially Molly. She adored her father and was always wearing his badge around the house, and she wanted to be a policeman too. Rose, on the other hand, was always hanging around me, especially when I was doing my makeup. She wanted me to make her look like me. It was so adorable, so I used to put lipstick on her and pretend to add eyeliner and face makeup. She would look into the mirror and right away exclaim she was beautiful!

On this particular day, I was not paying attention to my surroundings and hadn't noticed someone had been following me until he came up behind me and tapped me on the shoulder. I jumped about a mile and turned around.

"Please, don't be scared," he said while holding his arms out in front of himself. "I was a friend to Carlos, and I just want to give you this," he said while handing me an envelope, then quickly ran partway up the street, jumping into a car that was waiting for him.

I looked down at the envelope, almost afraid to open it. I looked around to see if I was by myself and then began to open it up. Slowly, I pulled out another picture of Johnny. This time he was smiling and standing, I presumed, by his grandmother. It had to be recent because he looked to be about six. The tears immediately went rolling down my cheeks as I smiled to myself—he is safe! I now had a difficult decision to make as to whether to tell Scott and Lieutenant Bickford. I decided to quit walking any further and head for home.

As I walked into the house, Scott asked me why I cut my walk short. It was then I decided to show him what was given to me even though he would be upset, but he needs to understand this brought me comfort and assurance Johnny was okay. Someone was out there helping me, but who?

"We have to call Lieutenant Bickford immediately," he said as he walked towards the phone.

"Why?" I asked him. "There is nothing I could tell him, and I didn't recognize this gentleman; I also couldn't identify the car he got into except it was white."

"Mac, there may be fingerprints on this envelope, and he has pictures of Carlos's friends he hung around with that you may be able to identify," he explained to me.

"Okay," I agreed reluctantly. I really wanted all this to end; I was tired of always being in a constant state of sadness. Now that I was sure that Johnny was safe, I hoped someday we would find each other, but until that time, I wanted to leave this place and go to New England to start a new life. I needed to give my full attention to my daughters, who are here with me now! Tonight, I will tell Scott that I would be leaving very soon, and he would be welcome to come to see us anytime he could. *Please don't fight me on this decision.*

"Get the girl's coats; we are going to the police station with this new evidence," Scott said, interrupting my thoughts—I obliged.

When we had returned home after being absolutely no help to the Lieutenant, I was exhausted. The girls were very well-behaved, which made both of us very proud. They fell asleep in the back seat on the way home. While I was preparing dinner, I put Molly and Rose in front of our TV set. *Was I a bad parent?* Scott went upstairs to shower because he was on the night shift this week and would be leaving after dinner. I was secretly glad about that and was looking forward to putting the kids to bed while being able to enjoy the evening alone. I promised myself I would tell Scott tomorrow after breakfast and before he went up to bed to sleep for several hours. Maybe I would take the girls to Fiona's afterward so we wouldn't disturb his sleep.

Dinner was quiet except for the occasional fussing between our two little cherubs. Scott spoke first after reprimanding Molly for teasing her sister. I will admit, though, Molly was a toughie, and Rose was the weaker of the two.

"Mac, make sure you keep the doors locked tonight and do not open it for anyone that you don't know and keep the outside lights on. I will call halfway through my shift to check on you. What time do you plan on going to bed?" he was very concerned about what had happened.

"I'm not sure; it depends if I get drawn into a good movie or not. Do you want me to let you know when I plan to *retire?*" I was being sarcastic. I truly thought he was overprotecting our daughters and me. "Scott, if that man wanted to hurt me, he would have done it then and there. He was delivering something to me that made me feel good inside. I am in no danger."

"Don't brush this incident off so easily. These men are truly dangerous; they mean business! Do as I say!" He then got up, kissed Molly and Rose, gave me a peck on the forehead and left. *Alone at last!*

I let the kids stay up longer than usual; I gave the girls a long bath and let them play for a while in the tub. When I was finished getting them changed for bed, which was truly a struggle, I calmed them down by reading their favorite fairy tales, and soon they were asleep. *Finally, alone!*

I then took a shower, got into my pajamas, and went downstairs to watch a little television. After a couple of hours, the phone rang; it was Scott checking in. I assured him I was fine and was about to go up to bed.

"Okay, double-check the doors, and I will occasionally drive by the house and check the outside." I rolled my eyes.

"If that is what you want to do. Thank you for keeping us safe, but I think you are going too far. I called Fiona tonight, and I will take the kids over to visit while you sleep tomorrow" I told him to have a safe night, then hung up and went to bed.

Chapter Thirty-Six

In the middle of the night, I woke up startled by a noise downstairs. It sounded like a chair moving. I glanced at the clock; it read four a.m.—too early for Scott to be home. I began to shake violently. *Was I imagining it!* Deciding to get up and check on Molly and Rose, I grabbed a flashlight from the dresser and tip-toed to their room. Peeking in and flashing the light all over, I saw that they were sound asleep. *Could I have been dreaming?* I went to the stairs and began the long walk down each step, being very careful not to make a sound. *What are you doing? Call Scott!* By the time I reached the bottom step, I had become very brave. After I checked the front door and turned on the outside light, I continued on my way to the kitchen and then the living room—nothing seemed out of place. I went to the back door—it was locked. I started to giggle to myself because I probably *had* been dreaming. I thought, *Silly girl!* I let out a huge sigh of relief when I realized nobody was downstairs. I went back upstairs to bed, where I quickly fell into a deep sleep.

Sometime later, I felt someone's hand over my mouth. Right away, I tried to scream; I began kicking the blankets and hitting and punching my attacker. *Oh, God!* Then I heard Scott's voice:

"Mac, Mac, wake up, you're having a nightmare! It's Scott; you're safe! You're safe. Stop screaming; you will wake the girls," he whispered in my ear.

My eyes flew open in terror, and I was just about to hit him again when I realized it *was* Scott. I glanced quickly around the room and knew I had a nightmare. Finally, I calmed down and put my arms around him; he hugged me tightly. "I, I, thought that man was in my bedroom and was going to kill me like he did Carlos!" The water-works turned on like a faucet.

"When I came home," he began, "I heard you were shouting to someone to get out, so I quickly flew up the stairs with my gun drawn and then saw you were beating up on no one." he smiled at me. I'm sorry if I put my hand over your mouth, but I didn't want you to wake Molly or Rose. Thank God they are deep sleepers," he added.

I pushed my hair away from my face and snickered. "I must have looked stupid."

I turned to look at the bedroom door—Molly was there. "Mama, Mama." she cried. I beckoned her to come to jump up on the bed and hugged her. Then we heard Rose *whimpering.* She was still in a crib and couldn't yet climb out. Molly was in a regular bed and could easily escape. Scott went into their bedroom and, within seconds, appeared at the bedroom door.

"Can we join you both?" he sweetly asked.

"Yes, you can, Daddy." Molly answered in her sweet baby voice.

Little did she know I was about to break their father's heart and take them both away. We all laid down together in bed until I decided to get up and make some breakfast for us all.

After we had eaten, I put the kids, again, in front of the TV to watch their favorite cartoons so I would have some time to talk to Scott before he went to bed. We were at the table finishing another cup of coffee he had made while I was getting the girls settled.

"Scott, I want to take the girls to visit Elsie and Alison for a while. I can't stay around here because I am worried about the safety of myself and the girls. I called my sisters, and they were very happy to hear that I wanted to take an extended visit to see them. You knew that eventually, that it would come to this," I told him while not looking directly at him.

"Yes, I was waiting for this conversation," he replied.

"Well?" I asked him. "Are you going to object to me doing this? I don't want us to get into any sort of legal battle. If I decide to stay there permanently, you know you can come to see them anytime, and I wouldn't object to the kids staying with you during one of the summer months later on when they are a little older. I just can't stay in this place any longer; there are too many bad memories here. I don't even know if I will like it up north, but I feel I have to give it a try." I then switched the conversation explaining the benefits of us separating before we began to hate each other.

He stared into his coffee cup. I felt bad for him because I knew how much he loved his girls, but we didn't love each other, and he needs to be with someone who truly loves him. I honestly thought that we both needed a new chance at life and to be in love. I care about him and will always appreciate everything he has tried to do for me. I truly believe he cares a great deal for me, but I know it bothers him that I can't let go of the past. He is really a great human being, and I was lucky he came into my life when he did—but it is time to let go.

As he got up out of the chair, he grabbed the dishes and put them into the sink, not even looking at me. As he started to leave the kitchen, he turned and told me he wouldn't object to me leaving. He also said he understood perfectly why I needed to go.

"I will take a few days off next week, and I will help you make your plans," he replied. "I'm going to bed now. Have fun at Fiona's." He then turned and went upstairs.

I felt terrible because I knew how horrible he must feel. Today, I will tell Fiona and Frank that I will be leaving. I just hoped that they wouldn't give me a hard time about this decision. My mind was made up, and no one would be able to change it!

Part THREE

"Fifteen Years Later"

Chapter Thirty-Seven

"I don't understand why I have to attend Rose's boring graduation ceremony!" Molly complained. "She didn't have to attend mine!"

"She was in the hospital having her *appendix* out!" I shouted at her. "You know she would have gone if she could." I was angry beyond words about Molly's selfishness. "Your dad is coming all this way to be with both of you during this special occasion, and you know that Rose struggled to get here; things were not as easy as it was with you, and being dyslexic was difficult for her, so stop acting like a child! You're going, and that is final." I was done talking.

Molly mumbled a few things and left the room in a huff. She really was a great young lady, but she definitely liked things to go her way. I was glad Scott was coming; maybe he would be able to talk to her. *Was Molly jealous of her sister?* These last fifteen years were difficult for us, but we had the support of Elsie and Alison, which had been a blessing.

I began to reminisce a little about when we arrived here. On the one hand, I was relieved to leave my old life behind, but I was afraid for the future. I had asked myself many times if I had made the right decision for my girls. Back then, I wasn't sure, but now I know that it was. We only stayed with Elsie for a few months before I bought a small house for the three of us. It wasn't much, but I made it into a cute and cozy home. I had quickly found a job as a paralegal for a small law firm. It was a husband-wife collaboration; they helped the less fortunate receive the justice they were due at a minimal cost—right up my alley. Every once and a while, they would represent someone who could pay what Dave and Margaret truly deserved to get for their hard work and exceptional knowledge of the law—I admired them so much.

Fortunately, for my children and me, they regarded us as family. After a few years, Dave approached me and suggested I go back to school to get my law degree, as he would eventually be retiring and wanted me to run his law office. I knew if I did something like that, I would be working and going to school at the same time. What would happen to Molly and Rose? I explained to both of them that I couldn't neglect my children in that way. It would mean shuffling them back and forth to after-school programs and babysitters. I wanted to be there as they grew up, just like my mother was for all her children. Mum was always there for us when we came home from school, and that was what I wanted my children to experience. He totally understood why I couldn't take him up on his offer.

I heard the doorbell ring and was suddenly startled back to the present day. *That must be Scott.* I quickly went and answered the door.

"Hey, you made it," I said to him with a smile.

"What a flight, lots of turbulence. I know you would have freaked." he grinned as I ushered him into the house.

"I made up the love seat in the den for you. How long are you staying?" I asked.

"About a week," he replied. "If that's okay with you," he added.

"Of course, it is. I'll be working most of the time, and I know the girls are looking forward to spending some quality time with you, especially Molly. It seems she has some things she wants to discuss with you and won't tell me what they are." I gave him a wink, picked up his suitcase, and brought it into the den.

"I have an idea about what she wants to ask me; she hints about things whenever we talk, and I know she thinks you will not agree," he grinned as he followed behind me.

We stood for a few minutes without speaking. "Well, are you going to tell me what you suspect?" I asked him. I was getting a little "hot under the collar," as the saying goes.

"I'm not going to tell you, but I will suggest to her that she needs to come clean with you before I agree to anything. I will say, though, I think she has made a good decision." He began to unpack some of his things and place them in a tiny cabinet that used to house old cassettes that I enjoyed listening to when I was alone. I temporarily removed them so he could use it as a dresser. "By the way, where *are* the girls?" he added.

"They are in their room. I'll tell them you are here." I said, walking out of the room. Sometimes he infuriated me the way he always looked at things so logically. I, on the other hand...

Rose came out of her room first, all dressed in her cap and gown with a very cute dress underneath. She was thrilled that her father had flown all the way up north for her graduation.

"Daddy, I'm so glad you made it," she screamed as she ran over to give him a big hug and kiss on his cheek. She still had a sweet little-girl tone to her voice.

"Wow, sweetheart, you look gorgeous." He returned the affection. "I wouldn't have missed this for the world."

"Daddy, you're here!" Molly ran to her father and hugged him around his neck. They exchanged secret glances, not knowing I caught the *look! Yup, she was up to something!*

"Rose has to be at the school early, so I will drive her now," I chimed in. "You two can discuss whatever it is you want to talk about while I am gone, but I want both of you to be ready to leave when I come back, though." I smiled and glanced at Scott. I couldn't wait to hear Molly's "great idea" that I wasn't going to approve of. *Two peas in a pod.*

The graduation was very nice. I think the three of us clapped the loudest when Rose accepted her diploma. The big surprise was Rose received a small scholarship she could use when she took her business classes online. Scott and I knew Rose would not be going to a regular college because she was determined to open her own hair salon/spa someday. This has been her desire since she was a small child. I am so proud of her, and I believe she will accomplish this goal. I only wished I had the money to help her start a business, but unfortunately, I had used up all the extra money my mother had given me when I bought our home. After we had taken Rose out to a very classy restaurant and had finally arrived home, Molly decided to steal the limelight and shock me with her news.

Chapter Thirty-Eight

"You want to do *what?*" I asked Molly in disbelief. I then glanced at Scott. "This is what you wouldn't tell me?" My eyes shifted back and forth between both of them. I was livid!

"Mom, be reasonable, I am nineteen, and Dad said it would be okay with him and that it was a great idea!" Molly pleaded.

Molly wanted to move back to Florida to go to the Police Academy and become a policewoman—I was dead set against it. It was too dangerous, I informed her. I looked over at Rose to see what her reaction was, but she had left the room. This wasn't fair of Molly and Scott to bring this up now; it was Rose's time today to shine. Once again, Molly has stolen Rose's thunder!

They had ganged up on me, which I didn't appreciate. We must have had a discussion that lasted a couple of hours—arguing both pros and cons of her decision—but in the end, I had to relent and tell her she could go. When we had finished our discussion, Rose came out of her room and lent her support to her sister. She told everyone to let Molly follow her dream and that she was happy for her—it was so like Rose to say that. Molly went up to her sister, hugged her, and gave her a kiss on the cheek in appreciation.

She took Rose by the shoulders and asked, "Are you going to miss me?"

"You know I will, Moll. Promise you will write a lot and also call us," she exclaimed with tears in her eyes.

Scott interrupted the girls before the conversation turned dramatic. He hated to see his daughters cry, and he feared that is where they were headed. "Look, Rose, you will come down and visit, and Molly will come back up here after her graduation from the academy. I will take good care of her, and besides, you are going to be busy with your work and school." He walked over to them both and put his arms around them. "You girls make your mother and me very proud," he added as he wiped his eyes.

"Daddy, are you going to cry?" they both said together, laughing.

Scott smiled, "Nah, not me."

That night we all sat down and planned everything out; Molly would have to leave with Scott and head back to Florida at the end of the week in order to get into the summer program. Otherwise, she would have to wait till fall. I would have preferred fall, but I knew Molly was anxious to start this auspicious beginning of her new life—a dream realized.

I went to work the next day and asked my boss if I could have a few days off this week to spend with Molly, Scott, and Rose. After explaining everything that had happened the night before, he was very supportive.

"Absolutely, my dear," he said to me without any hesitation. "I am so happy for Molly and the decision she has made. I believe she will be a success; you must be so proud of her," he added.

The next day, I helped Molly pack all her clothes that she wanted to take, and if there were other things, later on, I would just mail them to her. We also picked out things she wanted that were too heavy to take with her, so we packed them and sent them by mail to Scott's home. I contacted Fiona and Frank to let them know what was about to happen. They were all excited and couldn't wait till she arrived. Frank told me he would be on the lookout for an inexpensive car to give Molly when he saw her. Everyone was so excited about what Molly was about to embark on—everyone but me. We visited Elsie and Alison and told them of Molly's news. Each one wanted to give her money to help her get settled. *What a family I had.*

The following day, we all went to Boston to spend time together. I was just as thrilled as my daughters were. In all the years living so close to Boston, we had only been there maybe seven times. On the second day, we all decided to drive up to the Berkshires. The girls loved this day; we went to the Norman Rockwell Museum, Tanglewood, and ate at a fabulous restaurant. It was an exhausting two days, but it was worth it. Several times I stared at Scott as I watched him mingle and laugh with his daughters. I thought how I wished we had been madly in love and were still together; he truly was a great father and man.

"What are you thinking about, Mac?" he asked me, interrupting my thoughts.

I was honest with him, "That you are a great father!"

"But, not a great husband?" he chuckled a little.

I pushed him slightly and replied, "I wished things could have been different between us, but you know, and I know, we just weren't in love. We were more like good friends." He agreed with me and gave me a big hug as he told me I was a great mom.

The day before they were to leave, we just stayed at home and reminisced about when the kids were little. They didn't remember much, but they liked listening to how cute they both were. No one mentioned Johnny's name, for which I was glad. That was long ago, and I am okay now, even though some days he is all I can think about.

I couldn't sleep the night before they were to leave. I tossed and turned. I would miss my oldest daughter immensely but admitted to myself, life would be much simpler with just one at home—only one to worry about. I was positive Scott and *Kelly* would take good care of her. Scott had married my friend Kelly a few years after I left. They both swore that there was no hanky-panky between them until after I had been gone for about a year. Do I believe them? I'm not sure. It really doesn't matter now, anyway. He seems content, and they have a ten-year-old son, Seth. I was truly happy for both of them, and I only hoped that someday *I* would meet Mr. Right!

The next morning, we drove to the airport in silence. I was trying to hold my feelings inside because I didn't want Molly to see me cry. I think Molly sensed my heartache and leaned towards the front seat and told me everything was going to be okay.

"You know I will miss you terribly, Mom. I will do everything Kelly and Dad want me to do. Don't worry; I will concentrate on my classes and my training and make you proud."

I wanted to add "and no boyfriends!" I smiled at her and told her she has always made me proud.

Chapter Thirty-Nine

I was determined not to contact Molly; I wanted to give her some space. Finally, after one week, she called me. She was so bubbly and excited on the phone; she couldn't stop talking. Molly had told me she would be starting classes first and then would be doing physical training afterward.

"Mom, I miss you and Rose so much, but I am so gung-ho about the probability of becoming a police officer. I wish I really had your blessing," she said to me with hope in her voice.

"I've thought about everything, and yes, you have my full support. I know you will be a fabulous policewoman, and I am very proud of you," I replied. After our conversation that morning, I got dressed and went to work, expecting my day to go as usual, but as it turned out, it wasn't just an ordinary day for me...

No one was in the office yet when I arrived. I proceeded to check messages and separate the ones I could answer from the ones I had to delegate to either Dave or Margaret. The first message I could handle was from Jane, our receptionist. She was ill and wouldn't be in the office today. That will mean I will be the receptionist along with my regular duties. I looked at the appointment book and saw only two appointments: one for Dave and one for Margaret. That was a good thing because I had so much research to do for them both. As I turned the page to the next day's appointments, I noticed a piece of paper with the words Jack Foster scribbled in messy handwriting, which I recognized as Dave's. It listed a phone number and a note that this client would be coming in today at three with today's date on it. I just shook my head in confusion because I wasn't sure if Dave meant the gentleman would be in today or tomorrow since the paper was on the next day's page, and maybe Dave wrote the wrong date down. I shrugged my shoulders and penciled Mr. Foster in for today, and if he didn't show up, I would know Dave had meant tomorrow.

Dave was in court today till around two and couldn't be reached, and Margaret would be in just before her appointment at one. That would mean I had most of the day to myself, which I was very glad about because I had so much work to do. The morning was very quiet, with only two phone calls that resulted in two new clients for the Roberts to meet. Margaret came in promptly at one, we spoke for a few minutes, she took her messages, and then her client came in shortly afterward. Dave came strolling in at two.

I was sitting at Jane's desk, going through her calendar for the week so I could plan *my* week, when this rather tall older gentleman came strolling in. I glanced up at him and immediately felt a familiar flutter with my heart. *My first meeting with Carlos!* He was striking, though not all that good looking. He strolled over to the desk and told me his name was Jack Foster, and he had an appointment with Attorney David Roberts. I smiled at him and looked at his name that I had penciled in earlier; I quickly put a checkmark next to the appointment.

"Attorney Roberts is with his two o'clock appointment. Won't you please have a seat, Mr. Foster, and he will be with you shortly." I buzzed Dave to let him know his next client had arrived. Mr. Foster thanked me and sat down. After a few moments, while I was going through some depositions, I noticed a shadow in front of the desk. I glanced up at Mr. Foster and smiled at him. "May I help you?" I asked him politely.

He looked down at my left hand and then quickly replied, "May I use the restroom, Miss..." he hesitated.

I covered my left hand with my right and replied, "Miss Ables and the restrooms are down the hall on the right." I did notice he was not wearing any rings, but I knew that didn't mean anything because a lot of men didn't wear wedding rings for one reason or another. I watched as he walked down the hallway; he stopped and turned to look at me, then gave me a smile and walked into the bathroom. My head flopped down on the desk as I suddenly felt seventeen; I knew I was attracted to him almost immediately. I was relieved to find out I still could feel something for someone else.

After a few minutes, Mr. Foster came back into the waiting room and approached my desk. Again, I looked up and asked, "How may I help you?"

"They sure are making receptionists attractive these days," he said to me with a big grin.

It took me a minute to realize he was flirting with me. "Thank you, but I am not the receptionist. Jane is out sick today, so I am filling in for her. I am actually Dave's and Margaret's one and only paralegal, and I sometimes fill in when it is needed; thank you for the compliment, though." He seemed embarrassed. "And by the way, why would you think that receptionists are unattractive?" I added, smiling.

He began to stammer and stutter a little, trying to tell me he was only joking around. The more he talked, the deeper he was in trouble with me. I let him try to apologize; then I looked at him, and with a smile as wide as the room and a little chuckle, I told him I was just trying to make him uncomfortable and that I didn't mind what he had said at all. His shoulders dropped, and I could tell he was relieved. At that moment, Attorney Roberts came out of his office, said goodbye to his client, and quickly walked over to shake Mr. Foster's hand to introduce himself.

"I see you have met my right-hand-man; I mean woman." he smiled as he beckoned his new client (hopefully) into his office. Before he shut the door, Dave winked at me. *Did he pick up on the attraction?*

After about an hour, Dave and Jack came out of the room smiling. I knew right away by their demeanor that Jack had signed on to be represented by Roberts and Roberts. I would know soon enough why he sought their counsel. When Dave went back into his office and shut the door, I started to gather my things together because it was time for me to leave. Jack stood there at my desk and watched for a couple of minutes. I suddenly felt the heat quickly creeping up my whole face and knew I was blushing.

"I'm going to grab a cup of coffee next door, and I wondered if you felt like joining me," he said hopefully.

I looked up at him and then at my watch. "Sure, I would like that, thanks," I responded, trying to hold back my excitement.

"Great," he exclaimed while helping me pick up some of my folders I had to bring home to work on. "After you," he said, bowing his head as he held the door.

Chapter Forty

When I arrived home that evening, I was happier than I had been in a very long time. Jack had asked me if I would like to go out to dinner sometime with him. After the impressive conversation at the coffee shop, I decided to tell him I would be delighted to go out with him. He was quite different than the men I had occasionally dated during the last fifteen years. I had almost given up on ever being truly attracted to anyone.

He mentioned he bought old homes, fixed them up, and then flipped them (reselling them). He also bought land and built condos on them, though this was a recent endeavor for him. I found out he collected older motorcycles, and they were his true passion in life. I briefly summed up my life quickly without mentioning Johnny. I'm not sure why I didn't bring that time up in my life, but maybe it was because Scott never wanted me to constantly bring it up with him. He always preached to me that in order for me to move on, I needed to let go of the past, so that is what I have done. Jack also briefly told me he was divorced with one son. He never elaborated on it, though, and I didn't push him on any further information.

We made plans to go out to eat the following weekend. He mentioned he wanted to show me one of the houses he was stripping and re-decorating—get my opinion. I was excited to go out with him. While living in my very small home for over fifteen years, I was sure I must have re-decorated each room at least three times—decorating was *my* passion.

Within a few months of dating, Jack and I were almost inseparable. There were many times he stayed over because he lived about twenty-five miles from me. When we went out to a club to dance or just listen to a band we had liked, it was generally a very late night out. I was the first one to suggest he stay over because he had too much to drink on that particular date. Many times, he bragged to me that he had never been intoxicated in his life, no matter how much alcohol he had consumed. That was hard for me to swallow, and I thought he was just trying to impress me. I knew on that particular evening he had consumed at least seven drinks, and I couldn't, in good conscience, let him drive home. After that date, he always stayed over when drinking was involved.

Rose had moved out of the house and was living with a friend of hers. She worked very hard and was saving money so she would be able to start her own beauty business. Rose had almost no social life because she worked during the day and went to school, online, in the evening. I was very proud of her and couldn't believe how determined she was to go into business for herself. I had wished I could have helped her, but I didn't have too much money that I could part with right now.

One day, I was discussing this with Jack, and he suggested that he would gladly lend her the money she needed to buy into a business that was for sale near her home. I immediately put the brakes on that idea. Jack couldn't understand why I rejected his offer so vehemently.

"Jack," I started carefully, "for one thing, she is not anywhere near ready to take on something that complicated. You, of all people, should know what is involved in buying into anything. Please do not ever mention your offer to her," I finished sternly. He knew it was not open for discussion!

One day, during one of our dates, Jack said he had a surprise for me. He called it a ten-month celebration. I had no idea what he was talking about, but apparently, it was a special milestone to celebrate for him.

"You don't have to give me anything for staying together ten months," I told him while feeling a little cautious but curious none-the-less. He reached across the table and grabbed my hand.

"Don't worry, I'm not going to propose," he smirked. I smiled at him with relief. He then reached into his pocket as I held my breath and then pulled out an envelope and handed it to me.

"What is this?" I asked him suspiciously. He didn't answer me but swished his hand at me to indicate to just open it. As I began to open it up, I looked up at him, and he was grinning from ear to ear like a school kid who just brought home his report card with all A's on it. What I had pulled out of the envelope were two tickets to Hawaii. I was flabbergasted. "For, for us?" I stuttered.

"Of course, for us! Who else? Do you want to go or not?" he was so proud of himself. "I have already cleared it with Dave and Margaret." He was now on a first-name basis with the Roberts. They had handled many cases for him since their first meeting.

"I don't know what to say. Of course, I want to go. Are you kidding? I have never been there and didn't think I would ever go—not in a million years."

"Well, baby, pack your bags because we leave next week."

My head was reeling; I immediately knew I had some serious shopping to do—a bathing suit for starters. I stood up and went over to him just as he got up. We embraced and kissed while all the curious patrons looked on. I then shouted, "We're going to Hawaii!" Everyone began to clap for us—it was a memorable night.

Our ten days in Hawaii had been the best vacation I had ever taken. It was while we were there, Jack announced that he loved me with all of his heart, and he wanted to provide for me for the rest of my life. I was in total shock and didn't know what to say. He knew, and I knew, that neither of us wanted to ever marry again, so, what did he exactly mean by that statement? He suggested I sell my house, live with him, and give the money to my kids so they would have a great chance to fulfill their dreams and not have to struggle to make everything they wanted in life come true.

I had told him that was a *huge* step in our relationship; it required a lot of thought and planning. He understood why I was hesitant, but he knew he would be able to convince me. We left it at that and just enjoyed the rest of our time on the island.

Chapter Forty-One

When I had returned to work after an incredible and surprising trip, I received another shock to my simple life. Dave and Margaret were there to greet me when I came into work, which was very unusual because I was always the first one into the office, followed by Jane, and then, depending on their clients, the Roberts would wander in later. You can imagine my surprise to see Jane, Dave, and Margaret waiting for *me!*

"Good morning," they all said simultaneously.

"Good morning; what are you all doing here this early?" I asked skeptically. I glanced at Jane, who quickly lowered her eyes. *Something's up.* Dave spoke first:

"We all have to have a meeting, but first, how was your vacation?" he asked, looking at me.

"All I can say is that it was magical! We had a wonderful time, and I can't wait to go back someday." I then looked right at Dave and asked him what was up?

He led us into the conference room, which made me very nervous. Margaret beckoned us to sit down.

"Please tell me no one is ill!" I said very quickly.

Dave grinned and replied, "No, no, nothing like that. Don't worry."

"Then please tell me why we are in here!" I was getting upset at this point. He finally told us that he and Margaret were going to finally retire. They wanted to spend the remaining part of their lives traveling, and it had been a very hard decision to make because of Jane and me. They promised they would do everything in their power to find us other jobs.

"I am going to give the few clients I have left to another firm, and they have all been notified," he added.

"When did this happen?" I asked, getting emotional. *Did Jack know about this?*

"It was when you were away on your trip. Margaret confessed to me that she had always wanted to go to Hawaii and how come we had never gone. That's when we just started talking and realized we aren't going to get younger, just older," he chuckled. "We are both healthy now, and the time is right."

I got up from the chair and went over and hugged each of them and told them that I thought it was a great decision. Deep inside of my core, I was scared for myself; what would I do without a job? I hated the thought of starting over. *Take Jack's offer?* Jane stood up and announced that she had found another job with another law firm and not to worry about her.

"In two weeks, we will be shutting the company down and transferring everything to the new firm," Dave continued. "We will be pretty busy getting ready for this move, and I apologize for any problems this will cause for either of you. Jane, I am glad you have found another job so quickly. You have been an excellent receptionist, and I will write you up a superior recommendation."

The rest of the day, I spent organizing my research results and finishing up cases that were going to be transferred to the new firm. I wanted everything in perfect order so there wouldn't be any loose ends, and everything would be easily understood by everyone working on these cases.

When I arrived home from work, there was a message from Jack to give him a call. I looked around the house with sadness in my heart and thought moving in with Jack might be a good thing—maybe I will go back to school to get my degree. I called Jack, and he said he would like to come over, so I had about an hour to change and shower before he arrived. I decided to wait to see if he brought up the *moving-in thing* before I told him about the office closing—I didn't want charity!

When he finally arrived, I was in the kitchen preparing some pasta with chicken for our dinner. He mentioned on the phone about going out to eat, but I wanted to make him a home-cooked meal instead of us always dining out. That was one thing I didn't like about him; he had to always wave his wads of money around to everyone at restaurants—excessive tipping. I secretly thought he was really a very insecure person, and maybe he thought by letting people know he had money, he would be more likable; I was not impressed by wealth.

"This is the most delicious chicken pasta dish I have ever had," Jack commented while stuffing his face. "I never realized you were such a great cook," he added, grinning like a child.

"My mother taught each of us, brothers included, how to cook. She preached that it would come in handy one day." I smiled at him. "Of course," I continued with an air of haughtiness, "I am the most talented!"

"Glad to see you are so modest!" We started to laugh, and then he broached the subject of me selling my house and moving in with him. I was relieved that he was the one who brought up the subject of me moving in.

"Jack," I began seriously, "did you know that Dave and Margaret were going to close their practice and retire?"

"Yes," he confessed.

At least he was honest and direct. "Is that the only reason you want me to move in with you? Are you feeling sorry for me? Because if you are..."

He interrupted me, "No, absolutely not. I am in love with you, and I want you to live with me. Besides, you will make some money and can help Rose realize her dream of owning her own business and also help out Molly."

I thought for a moment, then I blurted out to him, "Let's do it!" I knew I probably should have discussed it with Fiona and my girls first, but I made this decision on my own, and if they didn't agree with it...

Chapter Forty-Two

By the next week, my house had been put up for sale, and within a month, it had been sold. We decided to put my things in storage till we could figure out what I would be putting in his home and what things he would take out of his place and either sell or store with my remaining things. The transition went very smoothly. I will say my girls were very accepting of my decision—not so with Fiona.

"You're going to do what?" she replied to my news over the phone.

If she could have reached into the phone, she would have choked me. Even after I explained everything, my plans for giving Rose money to invest in her business venture, she continued screaming so loudly that I had to hold the receiver away from my ear. Finally, she calmed down a little.

"Mac, you do not have a good track record for making good decisions. I was very proud of you after you left Florida and moved to New England. I thought that was a smart decision because of everything you had been through—to start fresh." She paused for a few minutes. "But this, this is the most irresponsible thing you have done. Why on earth would you sell your home, and what do you really know about this man?"

"I know enough. I am a grown woman now, not a teenager. I want happiness, and he makes me happy." I wanted to just hang up on her.

"I am coming up there to meet this wonderful man who makes you *happy!*"

Click, went Fiona's phone. I turned and looked at Jack. "She's coming." was all I said to him.

"Yikes!" was his response.

We had a lot of work to do before Fiona arrived. I wanted everything in order because I didn't want her to complain about chaos in the house. If there was one thing Fiona couldn't handle, it was chaos! Jack helped me as much as he could, but he did have to go to work every day. I loved where we lived; it was a small quiet neighborhood. His house, of course, was the biggest one on the block.

One afternoon, before the arrival of Fiona, my doorbell rang and scared the wits out of me because I wasn't expecting anyone. When I walked over and opened the door, a woman about my age was standing on the small porch with a pie in her hands. She introduced herself as Joanne, who lived two doors down from our house. Joanne had come to welcome me to the neighborhood. Even though I was in the middle of a mess, I invited her into the house. We talked for about an hour, and I had learned that she and her husband, Tom, were friends with Jack and that they both knew I would be moving in. Joanne was surprised when I admitted that Jack had never mentioned Tom or her before. I politely said that I was very glad she had come over, as I knew nothing about Jack's friends. Joanne then suggested we do lunch soon when I had the time—I agreed. *My first friend!*

After she left, I finished pushing furniture around in the living room until I was completely satisfied with the layout of the area. I had hoped Jack would approve because I was tired of struggling with heavy couches. I looked around the room and thought it looked very nice, but then realized that Jack might not like it. I just wasn't that sure about him. *I don't really know him!* The next room I tackled was our bedroom. I glanced at the clock and knew Jack would be home in another hour; I decided I would quit for today, take a shower, and then start dinner. Jack had mentioned he should be home around five, so I thought it would be safe to assume that five-thirty would be a good time to have dinner ready. Well, I assumed wrong...

It was seven o'clock when I decided to clean up the mess in my kitchen. *Where was he?* I was seething and tried to talk myself out of these feelings that were churning inside of me.

The least he could have done was to have the decency to call me! By eight o'clock, I was ready to just go to bed. As I climbed the stairs, I passed a mirror on the wall and stopped to look at myself for one brief moment. *Was Fiona, right?* Just as thoughts of an accident or illness suddenly crept into my mind, I heard the front door open and then closed very softly. I quickly continued up the stairs and went into the bathroom to get ready for bed. I did not want to know why he was home so late; I just was relieved he hadn't been in an accident or wasn't in a hospital. I pretended to be asleep when he finally decided to come upstairs to go to bed, and as soon as he entered the room, I knew he had been drinking because the smell permeated the room.

In the morning, I got up pretty early and could still smell alcohol as I left the room to go downstairs to have my breakfast. *Disgusting!* As I was eating and reading the morning paper, Jack came waltzing in as if nothing was wrong.

"Boy, I am so hungry," he replied without batting an eye. "I don't remember eating anything last night. What time did I get home?"

I slowly looked up from my newspaper. "Really? You don't remember?" I was furious at him.

"No, I don't." He innocently grinned at me.

"Sometime after eight, and you smelled of alcohol. I had dinner ready at five-thirty and waited for, at least, a call from you—but nothing!" I wrinkled my nose up at him while I cleared my breakfast dishes from the table.

"I'm so sorry," he apologized. "I was out with some friends, and I lost track of time. I want to talk to you about investing what money you have left. My friends were telling me about these investment opportunities, and they sound really great. What do you think?"

I told him it sounded like a good idea, but I didn't know much about the stock market, and I wanted to know if it was a safe thing for me to do. He remarked that this would be a sure way to make quick money and that he was going to invest in the same thing. I knew I only had about $20,000 dollars left from the sale of my house, and it wasn't making any money sitting in the bank.

We talked the rest of the morning about this venture, and finally, I agreed to do it. I thought that if he was going to invest, it must be okay; I knew he wouldn't part with money unless it was a sure bet! The next day, I went to the bank and withdrew my money, making the check out to Jack Foster.

Chapter Forty-Three

By the end of the week, Fiona had arrived. I was all ready for the fight I was sure would ensue, but there was no fight. Fiona remained calm and polite as she walked around the house, looking at everything. I was pretty sure she was pleasantly surprised as to what a nice home this was.

"When does Jack get home from work?" she asked while she took a seat at the table. I poured her a cup of tea and served some cookies I had made.

"He usually comes home around five," I replied, all the while hoping he wouldn't repeat what he had done a few days ago. I knew he didn't want to meet Fiona.

"Good, that gives us a few hours to talk." She crossed her legs then sipped her tea.

Her words made me cringe as I sat down while giving her my sweetest smile. "Okay, get it off your chest. I do not want you to show any animosity towards him when he comes home! I think you will like him or, at least, try to make an honest effort to see in him what I see." I took a deep breath and then continued, "However, he does have his faults."

"Well, why don't we start with those?" she snickered a little.

I gave her a few little things that irritated me about him but was very careful not to say anything that wasn't true for just about everyone. The rest of the time, I complimented him and made him an unbelievable human being: kind, generous, and caring. I also mentioned that Rose adored him. About four o'clock, Jack came home holding flowers that he handed to Fiona—right away, she was impressed.

Immediately, I stood up from the table to plant a kiss on his cheek and whispered in his ear, "Smart move!"

He suggested we all go out to eat somewhere to have a nice meal and a few drinks; I winced at those words. *Please, no alcohol!* I had failed to mention that fault of his. As it turned out, my worrying was all for nothing—he behaved impeccably. Jack only ordered a glass of wine, as did Fiona and I. It made me feel so proud of him, but I had planned on talking to him about his excessive drinking anyway after Fiona left to go home.

Fiona only stayed a couple of days, and even though she still wasn't totally convinced I should have sold my home, she admitted to me that she did like him. I was relieved to hear those last words from her, and when I repeated to Jack what she had said about him, he was relieved to hear it also.

"Now, can we move on without worry?" he playfully asked me.

"Yes, we can move forward, but I'm afraid it is not without some worry on my part. I want to discuss your drinking, Jack." I remarked with some hesitation in my voice. Unfortunately, that set him off.

"My drinking? Are you serious? Don't question me about my drinking; I am not an alcoholic!" He stormed out of the room like a child.

I yelled after him, "I never called you an alcoholic; please come back and talk to me!" He ignored me and went upstairs. I knew I had to try and fix this, so I followed him upstairs. "Jack, I am so sorry; I am just worried about you. Please talk to me." He was in the bathroom with the door shut. I kept begging him to come out and talk. Finally, the door opened, and out he came. I sat on our bed and asked him to sit with me. I thought he looked just like my brother had looked after being scolded by my father—a ten-year-old!

We talked for about an hour, and I explained what I had been seeing: late nights out, smelling of booze, putting vodka in his orange juice in the morning, having a glass of alcohol before bed, and bragging that he never gets intoxicated. After mentioning orange juice, he looked at me in total surprise. "Yes, I know what you have been doing," I confessed.

"So, what do you want me to do?" he asked. "I love you and don't want you to leave."

"Maybe you aren't an alcoholic yet, but I watched my uncle, my dad's brother, become one, and it wasn't pretty. I don't think I could deal with something like that."

"I have an idea," he said, changing the subject, "let's go on another great trip, and I will think about what you are saying. I thought of taking you on a Mississippi river cruise. Would you like that?" he smiled and winked at me.

Deep down, I was pretty sure he was just patronizing me. He wasn't taking me seriously enough. That is exactly what I *didn't* like about him. "Yes, that would be fun," I answered. I will give up for a while because it was no use arguing with him. I will see how he acts on our trip.

We planned to leave in a week. We would fly to Memphis, Tennessee, where we would board a small ship and then cruise down the Mississippi to New Orleans, LA. and then fly home from there—a total of eight days. It would be an exciting trip. Another incredible vacation that I would never have experienced in my lifetime had it not been for Jack.

On the day we were to leave, I received a phone call from Frank. He was very excited to announce that he was opening his third up-scale used-car lot, but it would be strictly classic cars from the sixties and seventies. He had a lot of work to do to get ready for this event and wanted to know if I would come to the opening in approximately two months. He had said it was going to be a big opening—he was going all out. Frank confided in me that it would be his last endeavor. Because of his age, he would be looking for someone to run the whole operation for him. He would oversee the three places but wanted someone else to be responsible for this new place. It was going to be quite a search for the perfect man or *woman,* he added quickly. I just laughed as I congratulated him, and I told him that Rose and I would be there. After the call, Jack and I loaded our luggage into the taxi, and off we went to the airport.

Chapter Forty-Four

When we had arrived back home, I was even more confused about Jack's drinking problem. He drank heavily all during our vacation, making me feel very uncomfortable. He bragged to everyone about his business, bought a lot of people their drinks, and tipping was another embarrassment I had to endure. At least, he was having a wonderful time and, of course, everyone loved him. *Mr. Smiles.* I had a lot of thinking to do.

During the next month, I noticed he wasn't drinking quite as much as he had been. He was, however, still adding alcohol to his orange juice in the morning and having a drink before bed, but his personality didn't seem to change during those times. I was somewhat satisfied with this little progress he was showing; he did seem to be trying. One particular day, about two weeks before Rose and I were going to fly to Florida for Frank's opening of his third car lot, Jack came home from work looking very disappointed and upset.

"Mac, I have something I need to tell you that you will not like. I did my best to avoid it, but the market is what it is, and there is not much you can do to change it." He sat down in the living room and beckoned me to sit beside him.

"What happened?" I was beginning to imagine all kinds of things in my head. I sat down beside him and turned slightly to face him. He reached for my hand, but I kept them both in my lap.

"You know that the stock market and investments can be volatile," he began carefully, "I'm afraid that the investments we made," he paused for just a second, "tanked!" He waited for my reaction.

At first, I had trouble getting the words out, and while raising my voice, I asked the question, "We lost it all?" I stood up quickly, "My $20,000 is gone?" Tears welled up in my eyes.

"Mac, I am so sorry; I lost what I invested also. Don't worry; I have several business deals I am working on, and I will help you get your money back. It might take a little while, but I promise I will make it up to you." He stood up and put his arms around me.

I told him I needed to be alone for a bit and asked that he not mention this to anyone else. God help me if Fiona or Frank got wind of this—yet another stupid thing that Mac did! *What is wrong with me?* I laid down on the bed and soon fell asleep. Before long, Jack came upstairs and woke me up for dinner, which he had made himself. He was truly upset about the disaster and apologized, over and over, for not pulling out beforehand. We had a long discussion over dinner, and he and I decided I would worry about it when I returned from Florida.

A few days after we had our talk, I noticed Jack was back to drinking quite a lot when he was home. *Here we go again!* I began to think that maybe it was me—is this what most guys do? I wouldn't be upset if it was just a beer can Jack was holding because I noticed Joanne's husband, each time he came to visit Jack, had a beer in *his* hand. Jack, though, was drinking hard liquor, not beer! I decided I would pay Jack's oldest friend Bill, who just happened to be his accountant, a visit. If I didn't get some insight into who Jack is or was, then I would go see his ex-wife! I knew she would be more than willing to tell me all about him. Maybe it wouldn't be the whole truth, but I would certainly get a little information on him. *Do I dare do this?*

As luck would have it, Jack told me he would be gone for a few days because he was going to look at some sland in New Hampshire that he thought would be perfect for the four luxury condos he wanted to build. This property was in an area that had nothing like what he wanted to build and was near Lake Winnipesaukee. He was very excited about his trip and said he would be gone for only two days and would be back in plenty of time before I left for Florida. *Perfect!*

*T*wo days later, he left. I was relieved because now I had plenty of time to see both Bill and Jack's ex, Karen, if need be. But first, I had to call my sister, Eileen, about our mother. Both Eileen and Bonnie wanted to put my mum in a nursing facility. They were feeling overwhelmed, as it was difficult to work, take care of their families, and watch over our mother. I understood but didn't quite know how to help them out. I really didn't want my mother to go into one of those places. I knew I couldn't bring her here because, for one, she would never do it. I was going to suggest they hire a nanny to take care of her, and then she could stay in her home. I would certainly chip in, and I am sure Fiona, Frank, and everyone else would help out financially. It was all I could think of for now. When I go to Florida, I will discuss any suggestions Fiona and Frank may have. Elsie and Alison both said they would go along with whatever we all decided.

I had called Bill to see if I could talk to him; he suggested we have lunch and talk then. That was perfect for me; I mentioned we could meet at one o'clock today. I would understand if he doesn't want to answer my personal questions about Jack's past. Bill is very protective of him, and I don't believe he would feel comfortable betraying his trust. They were both grade school buddies, and their friendship goes back at least fifty years.

Just as I was about to walk out the door, my phone rang. "Hello?" I asked anxiously.

"How are you?" Frank asked me. "You sound irritated; are you in a hurry?"

I told him I was fine, not wanting to let him know what I was up to. "I'm sorry, I was on my way out the door. What's going on? Is everything okay?" I was unsure why he was calling me.

"I am checking to make sure you and Rose are still coming next week? I have so many things going on and am very excited for you to be a part of it." he paused for a second, "You're not going to believe it!" he added.

I had the feeling he was holding back something. He usually isn't this excited about anything. *Marriage in his future?* I told him I wouldn't miss his *grand opening* for anything! Frank had been with his girlfriend for over fifteen years but had never mentioned marriage. They both were okay with their lifestyle, but maybe they have had a change of heart—I hoped so.

Chapter Forty-Five

My lunch with Bill was very enjoyable, but I never found out much about Jack's past. I was right about Bill not wanting to betray the trust of his friend. He did tell me I should ask Jack directly if I wanted to know anything. We both mentioned, though, about Jack's drinking. Bill thought he was drinking too much, which could eventually cause problems. I told him that I was working on it.

As soon as I left Bill, I headed over to see Karen. When I had talked to her earlier, she was more than eager to speak with me, and I didn't get a good vibe from her. I had decided that whatever she told me, I would take with a grain of salt because I could tell that she was still very angry with him. Within a half-hour, I arrived at her home. It was small but adorable. She had a good-sized yard, which was maintained beautifully. I walked up to the door and knocked.

Karen opened the door very quickly as if she had been looking out her front window for my arrival. "Hi, MacKenzie," she extended her hand. "Come in, won't you?"

I told her that it was very nice to meet her while following her into the living room. I instantly loved the set-up of the house. She definitely had a knack for decorating, which I mentioned to her. She seemed pleased that I would comment on her home. When I sat down, she excused herself and went into the kitchen area to bring back a tray of coffee and a few cookies and brownies. I really wasn't hungry and didn't want to be rude, so I thanked her for going to all this trouble, and while sipping my coffee, I picked up a brownie and started to nibble at it.

"MacKenzie, trouble in paradise?" she said sarcastically.

I thought to myself, "How much should I tell her?" "Well," I began, "I am mostly concerned about his drinking. I have been trying to get him to slow down, but he isn't very receptive to my suggestions." We stared at each other for a few minutes. I got the feeling she was thinking the same thing as I was—how much to reveal.

"I fought with him about that for just about all our married life— fifteen years. He went to A. A. for about a year, but unbeknownst to me, he stopped going." As an afterthought, Karen added, "He has other issues also; should I list them?" she ended with great satisfaction.

She seemed too eager; did I want to hear? "What else?" I asked cautiously.

She put her hand to her mouth, "Hmmm, where should I start?"

I was getting nervous; this was an angry ex-wife. "I don't need to know everything that went wrong with your marriage because the way I look at things, it takes two people to break up a marriage, and I will only be hearing your side." I wanted to be fair to Jack. "How about telling me something I may find out pretty soon anyway. I know you probably have been very hurt from something he has done, but I want to, at least, give him the benefit of the doubt."

"Sweet, sweet MacKenzie," she said with pity. "He is a habitual gambler and a great liar." At those words, she stood up and said we were done with our conversation.

As I got up to leave and thank her for seeing me, she had one more thing to add.

"Hold on to your money, honey." she smiled as she was shutting the door behind me.

I ran to my car and quickly hopped in. "What did she mean by that?" I spoke out loud. At that moment, I wished I had never spoken to her, or Bill for that matter. I can never let Jack know I went to either of them. I knew I could trust Bill not to say anything, but Karen I did not trust. *What have I done?*

All the way home, I kept thinking of the money I lost. I pounded the steering wheel over and over again. How could I be so stupid? I desperately needed something good to happen in my life! Where is Jack now? I wondered if he had lied to me. Damn Karen, why did I listen to her? She has placed so much doubt in my head. Had he been in A.A. for a year? Everything she told me was eating at my insides, and now I was really looking forward to getting away. *Florida, here I come!*

Jack was supposed to come home sometime this evening. How was I going to look him in the eye after what I did behind his back? He probably won't ever forgive me if he found out. Would Karen tell him that I came to her for information? At least, I will have a few hours to wind down before he comes home; I will have to pretend that nothing has happened. As I turned into our street, I saw Jack's truck! *He's early!*

My mind was racing, trying to think of what I would say if he asked where I had been. It turned out I didn't need to tell him. Karen had left a message for me on the phone. As soon as I opened the door, I saw Jack standing right there with his arms folded across his chest—he was not happy!

"It seems you left something at Karen's house!" his cheeks were beet red, and his eyes were wide and piercing, almost threatening.

I realized, at that moment, that I had left my purse on her couch. She had practically pushed me out the door, and I didn't have time to think.

"I can explain," was all I mumbled to him as I turned around to leave and go back to Karen's house.

"Hurry back because we have a *lot* to talk about!" Jack replied as he shut the door behind me.

He was definitely angry. I could almost see the steam coming out of his ears. I smiled for a minute because I was thinking of a cartoon character I watched as a child. *This wasn't funny!*

Chapter Forty-Six

By the time I had returned home, I had a plan in place. I was going to confess that I went to her to find out if she had a problem with him drinking. I would tell him I was very concerned about our relationship. I definitely was not going to tell him I also talked to Bill, nor would I tell him the other things Karen had said about him. I sat in the car for a few minutes, calming myself down and getting ready for God knows what!

I was leaving in a few days for Florida, so I was hoping I would be able to straighten everything out with us before I left. When I opened the front door, he lunged at me and pulled me into the house quickly. I screamed at him to let go of me; I could smell the booze on him. He walked me into the living room and pushed me gently on the couch.

"Explain yourself!" he shouted at me.

"Please calm down, Jack. I'm sorry I met with her. I think she is a very angry woman, and I didn't stay long. I just wanted to know how to deal with your drinking, that's all. She just told me you had been in A.A. for a while but then quit without telling her. I tried to defend you, and then she told me to leave and not to bother her anymore; that's all, honest." He seemed to calm down a little bit, believing me.

"I'm sorry I was rough with you," he replied, walking over to me. He held out his hand, and I grabbed it as he pulled me up from the couch. "You are right, I am drinking too much, and it is getting out of control. I will start going to A.A. if you want me to. I don't want you to go to Florida with this between us. You should have come to me and asked what exactly ended my marriage. I would have told you everything, and you certainly didn't need to sneak and talk to her. Are you sure that is the only thing she said about me? Karen is a lying witch, and that was one of the things that made me drink so much; I couldn't believe anything she told me." He held me in his arms and kissed me. I let him even though I shivered at his touch.

For now, we had mended some fences, but it definitely wasn't over. I wanted to know what she meant when she told me to watch my money! I would positively pursue this matter when I came back from my trip. The next day, after Jack left for work, I decided to do some laundry and start packing some things—I hated waiting to the last minute. I emptied my dirty clothes hamper and headed to the laundry room. After the wash cycle ended, I opened up the dryer and noticed all of Jack's clothes had never been put away. Jack and I always did our own laundry and put our own clothes away. He had been doing his own since his divorce, and he mentioned he preferred it that way; I gave him no argument.

I guess he must have forgotten they were in there, so I thought I would do him a favor and put his clothes away before he came home. I filled the basket and headed upstairs to our bedroom. After throwing the clothes on the bed, I began folding everything very neatly, just like he did. I opened up his top drawer and saw it was filled with socks and underwear. Everything was in neat order; it was so much more orderly than my drawers that I felt a little embarrassed. I then opened the second drawer where he kept his tee shirts—it was a mess. I decided I would fold everything and make it look as neat as the top drawer. I took his tees out and laid them on the bed to be folded correctly. Underneath the mess was a long wooden box. I looked at it and wondered if I should open it up because I had never seen it before. "Oh well," I thought, "I can't get into any more trouble than I already am."

I lifted the box up and put it on the bed. It wasn't very heavy, almost like it was empty. I stared at it for a minute and then picked it up and shook it—no sound. I kept it on the bed and kept looking at it while I proceeded to fold his tee shirts. All I could think of was the story about the girl who opened Pandora's Box and released all the horrors of the world. I had to chuckle at that myth, and in actuality, Pandora's Box wasn't a box at all; originally, it was a sealed vase.

I picked it up again and slowly peeked inside. *What?* As I removed the lid, I noticed there were many stacks of $100 bills wrapped together—I was now in a state of shock! "Where did this all come from?" I remarked out loud. I dumped all of the cash on the bed and started to count it. There was $30,000, and underneath the cash were some casino chips inside an envelope! *Watch your money, honey!* "Could some of this be my money?" I thought. Does he gamble at a casino? I was sick inside and didn't know what to do about it. I quickly put the money back into the box and put it in his drawer, then I messed up his tee shirts and threw them back over the box in a sloppy manner. I opened his top drawer and took out the sox I had folded and put everything in the hamper and ran downstairs, putting it all back in the dryer. I left my clothes in the washer and would take them out when Jack came home. Hopefully, he will not know what I had found. I decided that on the day I was to leave, I would take $20,000 and go to the bank and deposit that cash in a new account. I will get to the bottom of this!

I completely pulled this off. Jack had no idea I found his little stash. I was desperate to find out if this money was mine. Maybe he didn't even invest my money! I didn't know how to go about finding out if he stole my money, or was this money something he had won gambling, and it just happened to be what I had given him plus a little more.

On the day we were to leave, Rose came to our home because Jack was taking us to the airport. This was a bad time for Rose to leave her business; thank heaven she had a very reliable friend and partner to manage Rose's Beauty Salon. The salon had been up and running for about a month, and I was in awe of my daughter. She worked during the day and did her classes at night. She and Marie had four experienced employees working at the salon, and their client list was gradually growing. A big thank you to Jack for finding the perfect place for her to rent. The money I gave her bought all her equipment and will help her stay afloat until she gets established.

Two hours before we were leaving for the airport, I went upstairs and took my $20,000 and put it in my purse. I explained to Jack that I had to go to the bank and withdraw some extra money to take with me. I wanted to get back quickly and prayed he wouldn't notice the money was missing until I was long gone.

At the airport, we kissed briefly while he told me to have fun and that he loved me. He told Rose to take care of me, and he was sorry he couldn't go with us this time. We gave a final wave as we went around the corner and headed to our terminal. I was going to try to forget about everything and just enjoy myself—my money was safe!

Chapter Forty-Seven

Our flight was unremarkable; Fiona picked us up at the airport because we would be staying with Don and her. Now that Margo and Maria shared an apartment, Fiona had plenty of room for guests. Rose and I were excited that we would see Maria and Margo again—it had been a long time. We found out that Maria was engaged and would be married next year. That was exciting news, and we couldn't wait to meet Will. On the ride to her home, Fiona couldn't stop talking about her future son-in-law. She certainly was all wound up about our visit also. We asked about Frank's new place, and why, this time, he was throwing such a big bash.

"I don't really know, but I will tell you that this will be his last place because he is thinking of retiring, and he found the perfect person to fill his shoes. I think Frank mentioned to you that this place is different from the other two. He will be selling and restoring cars from the sixties and seventies. The young man that he hired is young, but he can take apart an old car and put it back together like nothing." She turned towards me and touched my nose gently with one finger—I suddenly missed our mother.

As we turned into her street, we started to get excited. Don, Margo, and Maria were standing in the front yard waiting for us to arrive. As we got out of the car, Fiona pulled me aside and asked why Jack didn't come with us. I told her that it was a long story, and I would tell her after all this was over and before I headed home. She looked at me in surprise.

"Whatever you say. This is going to be a fun time, so I understand that whatever you are going through, you want to forget about it for now and just enjoy yourself," she said, comforting me.

"Thank you, now let me hug and kiss my nieces." I smiled as I ran to them.

Fiona had planned a big meal for dinner. I noticed there were two extra seats at the table, so I asked her who else was coming? She just told me that I would see soon enough. *So mysterious.* During the afternoon, we all caught up with everyone's life happenings: laughing and joking about when the kids were young. It was a very relaxing and enjoyable day; I had almost forgotten about what was probably brewing at home.

Just as Maria had finished telling her story of how she had met Will, her fiancé, the doorbell rang. Fiona asked me to answer it for them. I went to open the door, and there stood Molly in her uniform and Scott standing beside her. Tears streamed down my face; I couldn't have been happier. I gave them each a big hug and kiss and invited them in. As we walked into the living room, I gave Fiona *a* look. I knew I would see them both at the open house tomorrow, but this was a pleasant surprise seeing them while it was quiet and intimate.

"Where is Kelly?" I immediately asked Scott.

Before he spoke, he looked at Fiona, then me. "Well, Kelly and I are getting divorced, but now is not the time to discuss *my* problems. How are *you*? You look fabulous," he remarked, changing the subject quickly. I stared at him and mouthed the words *later* to him. He smiled at me and gave me a hug. Soon we were all sitting at the table devouring everything that Fiona had prepared for us. The food was delicious, as always. Since I had been a young girl, I had envied the fact that Fiona cooked just like our mother and actually enjoyed doing it—not me, though. I was more like my father; I would rather go out to a restaurant than prepare something to eat at home. Of course, I could cook, but I didn't love it.

When everyone had finished eating and the dining room was cleared of all the dirty dishes and leftovers were put in the refrigerator, Scott suggested we all play a game called Charades because this was a game he played with his family as a child. Fiona had written down on small pieces of paper every movie title she could think of and put them in a bowl for each of us to pick from when it was our turn. We all picked teams with Scott and me as captains. Each team member had to act out the title without talking and try to get their team members to guess the name of the movie within three minutes. We played for about two hours, and it was great fun except when my team lost. I was teased by everyone for the rest of the evening because we lost on my last turn.

Fiona excused herself and went to the kitchen bringing back her home-made apple pie topped with ice cream. Everyone was excited, as there was nothing like Fiona's apple pies. While eating, I looked around at my family and felt very fortunate to have the kind of family I had. When I finished my dessert, Scott suggested that the two of us go for a walk. I replied, a little too eagerly, that it was a great idea, and I would love to go for a stroll. We grabbed our light jackets as there was a slight chill in the air. During our walk, Scott asked me about my *friend* I was living with. I told him that I met him just before I left my job, and after about six months of dating, I sold the house and then moved in with him. I waited for the criticism—it didn't happen.

"Are you happy?" he asked me.

I hesitated a bit because of what had been going on. I was afraid to tell him the truth, so I lied and said everything was wonderful, but I wasn't positive it was love that I was feeling. I was pretty sure he could see through my facade, though. I then changed the subject and asked him point-blank about his up-and-coming divorce!

He grabbed my hand as we walked. "You know, Mac," he said while squeezing my hand, "after you left me, I was lonely. Kelly was there for me, and I didn't want to be alone, but it was never real for me. I never wanted you to go, but I knew you weren't happy, and you couldn't let go of your past. I didn't want to stand in your way because I knew you would never heal if you had stayed. I was crushed that you took my two little girls and left. Thank God, everything between us was amicable. It was tough," he continued, "but I flew up north to see my girls as much as I could and was grateful that you allowed them to come and stay with me most summers." We stopped walking, and he turned to me. "I have never stopped loving you." All of a sudden, he leaned down, took my chin in his hand, and gently kissed me. *I am confused!* After the kiss, we headed back to Fiona's. At the end of the evening, Scott thanked Fiona for a wonderful meal and then gave us all a hug and told us he would see us tomorrow at Frank's celebration. I followed them out the door to their car, and as Scott started to get in, I grabbed his sleeve and asked what the kiss meant. He grinned at me then promised we would talk before I left to go home.

"I enjoyed our walk!" he said while getting into his car. With a wave of his hand and a smile, off they went. I stood there throwing kisses to Molly and watched until I could see the car no more. I walked back into the house and looked at Fiona—she sensed something happened.

Chapter Forty-Eight

I walked into the main lobby of Frank's new establishment. He certainly went all out with the decorations because there were hundreds of colored balloons, flags, and a large table in the center of the room displaying all kinds of goodies. What caught my eye first was a fountain in the middle of the table with chocolate flowing from it into a large bowl. On each end of the table were bottles of champagne, wine, and non-alcoholic beverages—something for everyone. The room was very crowded; a lot of the people were strangers to me. It was very evident that Frank had gone a little crazy with this opening as opposed to the other two. Everyone was smiling and seemed to be looking right at me. *What is going on?* Rose left my side and went looking for Frank—where *was* he?

While I stood there taking everything in, a young man carrying a small child in his arms approached me. *Who was this young man?* As I looked closely at his eyes, my body began to shake. He then spoke to me.

"Mom, I would like you to meet your granddaughter, Carly," he smiled while waiting for my recognition.

Mom? At that moment, the room began to spin all around me, and I suddenly recognized his smile and his dark brown eyes as I began to slide gently to the floor. Before I lost consciousness, I uttered his name, "Johnny?"

The next thing I knew, I was in Frank's office lying on his couch while Rose was gently applying a cold face cloth to my forehead while calling out my name. "Wha.., what happened?" I asked, barely remembering anything. "Am I dreaming?" I said as I frantically looked around the room for Johnny.

"You passed out, mom, but you are okay now, and no, you weren't dreaming," she said, grinning. Molly, Scott, Fiona, and Frank were gathered around me, and in the corner of the room, Johnny stood with his wife and my granddaughter, Carly, which I presumed was named after his father, Carlos. When I sat up, Johnny came over and hugged me.

"I can't believe what I am seeing. How? When?" I had so many questions. "Where have you been?" I whimpered.

"Mom, when I was about six, I was told you had died in a tragic car accident when I was around six months old."

I stood up from the couch, and that was when the tears exploded and were uncontrollable.

"Johnny," I began while squeezing him tightly, not wanting to ever let him go. "I have been looking for you all these years, and I have never once given up on finding you. I have so many questions, and I want to know everything, every moment that you remember. Where have you been all these years?" I repeated.

Frank interrupted me, "Mac, he will tell his story later after the party because there are many people out in the lobby concerned about you. We need to go out there and celebrate. I still want to officially introduce Johnny as my nephew and my new manager." he said while looking at Johnny.

I glanced over at Johnny's beautiful wife and child—my daughter-in-law and granddaughter. Johnny motioned for them to come over to me, so I could be formally introduced to them.

"Mom, this is my wife, Margaret, and of course, Carly Mac Garcia," Johnny announced proudly.

I was very proud that Johnny gave Carly my nickname as her middle name. It sounded perfect, and I loved hearing him call me mom; I reached out to Margaret and gave her a hug and then asked if I could hold Carly. Of course, she answered with a yes. I carried my grandbaby in my arms out to the lobby. When we all entered, everyone clapped. I made a short speech telling everyone that I was fine and that this was one of the happiest days of my life. I looked at Molly and Rose because I wanted to include them in the other two times that were my happiest. They understood as they both gave me their biggest smiles. Before Rose and I had arrived, the guests had been told a short version of what had happened so long ago.

Frank quickly stood in front of the podium and quieted everyone down as he thanked them for attending this monumental occasion. He proceeded to list a special thanks to everyone who made this day very special, and he added he couldn't have done it alone. After introducing Johnny, Margaret, and little Carly, he began pointing out his nieces and his siblings and gave honorary mention to our mom and also his sisters and brother who couldn't be there.

The celebration had been a success; everyone had a terrific time and feasted on the food and drinks that were offered. Gradually people started to leave after a couple of hours. All I could think about was Johnny's journey up to this point and how he happened to apply for a job at this particular place. My many questions were still whirling around in my head as a fall wind storm did to the dead leaves on the ground. Once all the guests had gone, the rest of us, our family members, helped clean up. I was now surrounded by all the people I loved—I tried to relax.

Johnny and Frank drove three of the special automobiles from the garage back into the showroom for opening day on Monday. One was a navy blue 1965 Ford Mustang convertible. It looked brand new. The other two were Chevrolets: a 1964 Impala Super Sport and a 1965 Chevelle Malibu Super Sport, all had been refurbished. He still had a 1968 Chevrolet Camaro that was being worked on in the garage—his first customer-owned car. Frank and Johnny had high hopes for their business. They had gotten many inquiries.

Don arranged all of the chairs in a line so we could all sit and hear Johnny's life story up to now as was told to him by his grandmother and the things he had actually remembered himself. I was so excited about this moment; I waited a long time to hear what had happened after Carlos took him away from me, and hopefully why?

When we were all settled, Johnny got behind the podium and began his story...

Chapter Forty-Nine

"Johnny's Story"

"*I have never been the center of attention in my life. I am doing this so I may give my beautiful mother closure to a truly nightmarish time in her life. Mom, I hope everything I am about to tell you will answer all of your questions. Of course, I don't remember many things about my earlier years as a preschooler. That particular time in my life, my grandmother, Bernita Garcia, had to tell me about. She passed away a year ago, just before Margaret, Carly, and I came to America. Before I was born, she had divorced my grandfather, left Cuba, and moved back to Mexico, taking back her maiden name of Garcia.*

I was told by my Lita, which is what I called my grandmother, that my father brought me to Mexico to see if she could take care of me because my mother had been killed in a car crash—I was about six months old. My father had to go to work to support me, and sometimes, he was gone a week at a time. I only saw him a couple of times a week until I was about three. I never saw him again after that. My Lita confessed to me when I was much older, that she thought he was doing something illegal, that is why my last name was changed to Garcia from Perez.

When I was around ten, my uncle, Dad's brother, took me under his wing and taught me everything about cars. He always told me it would come in handy once I was older. I also was given a picture of my mother, me, and my dad. Supposedly, it was the only picture of the three of us, and I have kept it safe since that time. It is my understanding that my father gave orders to Lita to take a picture of me once a year on my birthday and send it to a certain person, which I found out was Fiona, every year. My grandmother did it for a while and then stopped. I'm not sure why, sorry.

When I was a teenager, I got a job at a resort in Mexico, not far from where I was living, doing odd jobs around the grounds. It was there I met Margaret. She and her parents vacationed at the resort every year, and the first time I laid eyes on her, I was hooked. We only had a week every year, but it was powerful. When she was old enough, she got a job working there in the summer, and that is when we fell in love. We married, and a year later, Carly Mac was born. I'm sure, Mom, you have figured out the reason why she is named Carly Mac. It was the least we could do for my parents.

After my Lita passed away, I decided I would go with Margaret and move to America. We settled in Arizona, near her parents. I had always wanted to go to Florida because I had hoped I would be able to track down my dad or at least find my mother's family. I had found Fiona's address among my grandmother's things. My sweet Margaret was excited about the move, her parents, not so much. After some convincing, they told us they wouldn't give us a hard time.

That brings me to how I found Frank. One day, the three of us were just walking around, looking at the neighborhood because we had just rented a condo down the street, and I knew I had to find a job as soon as possible, as we only had a small amount of money. It was just plum luck that we walked by this place and saw the small billboard with an advertisement for a manager. It described what kind of a dealership this was going to be, which was right up my alley because I had rebuilt many older vehicles with my uncle. I knew everything about antique cars. Margaret was a little apprehensive because she thought they would think I was too young. I told her, if they did, maybe I could work in a different capacity. I didn't care as long as it was steady work.

She waited outside with Carly and wheeled her up and down the street. I walked in and immediately saw Frank and went over to his desk. He looked up at me and asked if he could help me in some way. I explained to him that I was here about the job of manager. I thought he was going to laugh at me, considering I could tell he thought I was young. Instead, he opened his drawer and pulled an application form for me to fill out. He handed me a pen and got up, and told me he would be right back. Well, I filled it out, and while I was waiting for him to come back, I glanced at the pictures he had on his credenza. That's when I saw he had the same exact picture I had of the three of us in my wallet, which made me curious.

Finally, Frank came back, and I handed him my application, which he studied very carefully. When he finished, he looked up at me and told me he was very impressed. At that moment, I felt very proud of myself. I asked him if he thought I was too young for the job, and he told me not necessarily, but he did want to see me in action. I still hadn't mentioned the picture yet. He stood up and asked me to follow him to the garage while mentioning that he and his foreman were having a little trouble with a 1968 Camaro carburetor—nothing they did seemed to fix the problem; I was feeling pretty good at that point. After tinkering with it for about fifteen minutes, the motor quickly started; I think he was very impressed. He extended his hand and said I had the job, then we went back to his desk and talked about salary. It was after that I mentioned I had noticed the picture with the small infant with his parents on his credenza. He picked up the picture and told me it was his sister and her boyfriend, who is now deceased. I froze at the mention of my dad being deceased. Then I pulled out the picture I had folded in my wallet and showed it to him.

He was shocked and asked what my real name was. I told him it was exactly what I wrote on the application, John Garcia, but everyone called me Johnny. I also added that my mother had passed away when I was six months old from a car accident. Frank said his sister was very much alive and living up north. Then he told me the story of how my father took me without telling anyone, and the police had been looking for me for over twenty-two years. I was shocked to find that my father had been murdered and no one knew where I was. The more information I received, the happier I was that you, mom, were alive.

Frank mentioned that everyone thought I had been taken to Cuba, and Carlos's last name was Perez. I'll never forget that day. We talked for hours, and he told me we were going to surprise you, mom, by having a big celebration. I hope you weren't mad that we kept it a secret from you for a few weeks."

Chapter Fifty

I slowly rose from my chair with everyone else following my lead. We were all spellbound after hearing Johnny's story, and most of us had tears in our eyes. Johnny was first greeted by Margaret, who gave him a kiss and rubbed his back. She must have realized how hard this had been for him. I immediately went over to him and gave him a kiss and a huge hug—soon everyone had surrounded him. *God, he looked and acted like his father.*

When we were all ready to leave for the evening, Johnny approached me and asked if I wanted to stay with them at the condo for a few days to get to know Carly and Margaret a little better. I was ecstatic, and of course, I told him I would love to do that. Rose had to leave and go home to get back to her business and was very sad to have to leave in the morning. Elsie and Alison were leaving with Rose in the morning also. I was only staying a week because I had to go home to face the music. I was surprised I hadn't heard anything from Jack—he must be livid! Before we left, we made plans with Molly and Scott to meet for breakfast in the morning after they returned from dropping off Rose and my sisters at the airport. I can't explain what I was experiencing at that very moment.

I sat in the back seat with Carly on the way to Fiona's house to retrieve a few overnight things. She was truly an adorable one-year-old little girl. The three of us tried to get her to say, Nana, which was what I wanted her to call me, and I was determined to get her to say it before I went back home. *Home? Do I even have one to go to?*

*T*he week went by quickly, but at least I was able to feed, change, bathe and play with my grandchild—we bonded quickly. I also saw that Margaret was a terrific mother to Carly, and more importantly, she was a wonderful, caring wife; Johnny was very lucky. Soon, it was almost time to leave everyone; it was a sad end to the most exciting week of my life. We made tentative plans for them to come up north to stay for a week very soon. I did not tell anyone, however, what was going on in my life right now, not even Fiona. Somehow, she must have forgotten our little talk earlier, so it was just as well. On the last day before I was to leave, Scott asked to take me to the airport; he wanted some alone time with me. I had known what he was going to discuss because of the kiss between us and also what he had said to me. *Was I ready for this?*

*A*fter supper that night, I asked Johnny if I could borrow his car to go over to say goodbye to Fiona and Don. What I didn't say was I had something important to tell Fiona, and I wanted her advice.

"Of course, take your time." There was that Carlos smile. Every time I looked at him, I couldn't believe he was my child. He looked and talked like Carlos, but he had my fair complexion—what a combination!

"I won't be long, I promise." I blew them all a kiss as I went out the door.

On the way over, I rehearsed what and how much I was going to reveal to Fiona. If I tell her too much, she will begin criticizing me—*blah, blah, blah!* I did not want to hear it. I finally decided to just talk about the drinking and not mention the fact that I thought Jack had stolen my money, nor that he was a heavy gambler. I knew I would not be staying with Jack when I got back; I had decided to end it.

Before I pulled into her driveway, I noticed Frank's truck in the front of the house. I was glad because I could say goodbye to him in person instead of saying it on the phone later tonight, and I wanted to also thank him again for the celebration last week for Johnny and me. As I got out of my car, the front door opened, and Frank stepped out. As soon as he saw me, he came right over and gave me a hug and kiss and wished me a safe flight.

"Are you leaving now? I was hoping we could all chat for a few minutes. How is Johnny working out?" I asked him.

"Mac, he is such a smart guy; you should be very proud of him. His grandmother did a great job raising him. I can tell you, when I first found out that he was my nephew, I was so shocked. It was very difficult for me to keep it a secret for those three weeks from you. Now you can get on with your life and enjoy it. By the way, how is Jack? I was sorry I didn't get to meet him. When Fiona came back that time she went to visit, he had won her over."

Fiona stuck her nose out the door and shouted to us. "Hey, what is the hold-up? Frank, I thought you were in a hurry to get home?" she smiled.

Frank waved to her and quickly mentioned to me he had errands to do before going home. "Keep in touch, sis. I will call you when you get home. Love you." Frank then got into his truck, blew me a kiss, and left. When I went into the house, Fiona quickly asked what was going on with Jack and me. I sat down on her couch and began to tell her about the problem Jack had with the *bottle* and what did she think I should do?

She was very shocked. "I can't believe it. When I was there, he hardly drank anything. Are you sure he is as bad as all that?" she questioned.

I then decided to tell her everything. I let it all out, even the part where I went to his ex-wife and to his close friend, Bill. "I have decided, Fiona, that I have made another big mistake, and please do not lecture me. I realize the mistake I have made and decided I am leaving him as soon as I find a place to stay." She stared at me for a moment before replying. I could visibly see the wheels turning in her brain while organizing her thoughts carefully before responding.

"I won't lecture you or criticize you. I love you, and we all make mistakes, but enough already!" She smiled and gave me a little shove and a hug afterward. "I am just trying to lighten the mood a bit. I can't imagine what you have been going through. I thought he was perfect for you."

"I did too, but when I found that money, I almost dumped everything that was his all over the bedroom floor. I am going to allow him to explain himself, but if I can't trust him... I really don't want to have to deal with anything because apparently, according to his wife, Karen, he has been trying to stop his drinking and gambling for the last twenty years!" I got up from the couch and added, "Now that I have Johnny back in my life, I deserve happiness. My future with Jack will only bring more heartache."

"I think you are making the right resolution," Fiona replied.

Chapter Fifty-One

As Scott and I drove to the airport, I could tell that he had a lot he wanted to discuss with me. I, unfortunately, was not in a good place because I was thinking about what could be waiting for me when I arrived home. Before he even mentioned anything about his kiss, I put the brakes on the subject.

"I know you want to discuss the *kiss* and the fact you told me you still loved me, but I have something I have to face when I get home that I am not looking forward to. In fact, I am scared out of my mind. I have no idea how it will turn out, so I want you to put a hold on our talk for another time" I looked over at him and could tell he wasn't pleased. "I can't discuss it with you right now, but I am hoping you will understand," I added.

"If you have gotten yourself in some sort of trouble, maybe I should buy a ticket to fly home with you, and we can face it together," he said, grabbing my hand.

My God, how wonderful is he being? "I really can't explain my feelings. I have made so many mistakes, and I don't trust my choices anymore. I think I would be better off going back to England for a while and helping take care of my mother. I truly believe that is what I need right now," I explained. We barely spoke the rest of the way to the airport. Upon our arrival, I suggested he just drop me off in front of my terminal; he didn't need to come in with me.

I thanked him for everything and kissed him lightly on the cheek. As I got out of the car, he squeezed my hand and told me to be careful. I smiled, grabbed my luggage from the back seat of the car, and waved goodbye as I walked into the airport.

My flight home was almost unbearable. There was a lot of turbulence caused by the bad weather up the coast. I tried to sleep, but I was afraid something awful would happen, so I just hung on to the armrests until my knuckles were white. Finally, we flew beyond where the storms were and made it to Boston. *How will I ever fly to England after this ride!*

*R*ose wanted to pick me up, but I told her I would just as soon go by taxi. I knew when I had arrived home that the confrontation between Jack and me was going to be awful, as he sometimes had a temper if he had been drinking too much. On the ride in the cab, I practiced how I would handle the conversation about everything that I had done behind his back—this was not going to be easy!

When the taxi stopped in front of the house, Jack's truck was nowhere in sight. I was relieved. I paid the driver and thanked him, took my luggage, and put it down on the porch while I fished for my keys. As I stuck my key in the lock, the door opened without turning the key—it was unlocked! I stepped inside and stood there with my mouth wide in amazement. The inside of the house was empty; everything was completely gone. I sat on a piece of my luggage and started to laugh and then began to cry. After a few minutes, I went into all the other rooms, and there was no furniture anywhere. *Where were my things?* I decided to call Rose and ask if I could stay with her, and I would explain later. I then called Joanne, my neighbor and friend, to see if she knew anything. She explained to me Jack had told her that he and I were moving, and Joanne admitted that she thought that was strange because I had never mentioned anything like that to her before I left for Florida.

"What are you going to do now?" she asked with concern in her voice.

"I am going to Rose's home, and then I am heading to England to help take care of my mom. If you find out anything, or if Jack comes back for any reason, please ask him to get in touch with me; I would really appreciate it."

My next step was to call the storage place that housed some of our belongings that we didn't need now. We were going to figure out what to do with our excess furniture at a later time. I believed that everything was in my name and should be safe from him. After calling, the owner replied that no one had tried to claim any of the items in the storage unit. I told him under no circumstances was he to let Jack take anything out of there. He made a note that I had called and said he would keep an eye on that unit. I called Yellow Cab and asked to be driven to my daughter's apartment in Bedford, Mass. It was going to be expensive, as it was thirty miles away from where I was, but it would be worth the expense.

When I had finally arrived at Rose's, she came running out to greet me as I was getting out of the cab.

"Mom, what is going on?" She was very anxious.

"Let's go into the house, and I will explain everything. Have you spoken to your father?"

"Yes, he wanted to know if I had heard from you, and I told him that you were coming to stay with me for a while and then flying to England to take care of Grandma. He wants you to call him immediately when you get here." She sounded breathless and then continued, "Mom, I think he still loves you," she rambled quickly with a hopeful look in her eyes.

I didn't exactly know what to tell her because I had no idea what my feelings were. We walked into her living room and sat down together on the couch, and I knew she was becoming anxious about what I was about to say. I remained calm as I began to explain the predicament I was in, and when I had finished, I physically had to reach over and close her mouth.

"I can't believe what you are telling me; he seemed like the perfect guy, and I liked him immediately." she managed to choke out while she put her arms around me and whispered that she was so sorry.

"Please don't feel bad for me, I basically think people are good, and so it is hard for me to believe otherwise—I trust everyone. *No more, though!* I am now going to call a booking agent and have them find a non-stop flight to England, and hopefully, I will be able to fly home in the next day or two because your grandmother is very ill and needs me just as much as I need her!" It didn't take long for them to find a direct flight to England—I would be leaving in two days.

"Are you going to call Dad?" she asked hopefully.

"No, and you aren't either," I replied as I headed for the bedroom. "I'm going to lie down for a bit."

Chapter Fifty-Two

When I wasn't dozing during my long flight, I reflected back on my life. I guess I was trying to see what I could have done differently. Every mistake that I thought I had made had something good come out of it; so, how could it have been a mistake? Meeting Carlos, gave me Johnny, meeting Scott, gave me Molly and Rose, and Jack, well, there had been nothing good about that relationship except I was able to travel to Hawaii and also take a river cruise down the Mississippi. I chuckled to myself, thinking back—wasn't that a good thing? Were those things my silver lining? Thinking of Jack made me wonder where he had gone. I knew he had a son, but I didn't remember how far away he lived. "Would Jack go to him?" I thought to myself.

Thankfully, it was a smooth ride with no turbulence whatsoever. The closer we got to England, the more anxious I became because my sister, Eileen, was not very clear on just how ill my mother was exactly. Finally, we arrived at Gatwick Airport, and as the wheels touched down, tension left my body. Now I had to find a taxi to take me to my mom's house where Eileen and my brother, Danny, would be waiting for me. Bonnie would not arrive till the weekend.

I had not been home in a few years, and as I walked into the house, all my memories of my childhood came rushing at me. When no one greeted me at the door, I began to get a funny feeling in my stomach. I heard noises upstairs and thought it sounded like someone was crying. I was just about to call out to Eileen and Danny when down the stairs they came, and I knew by the look on their faces and the tears in their eyes, my mum was gone.

I was very angry at myself for not being able to get here in time and tell her how much I loved her and that everything was going to be okay. The next few hours were unbearable for Danny, Eileen, and me because we had to watch our mother being wheeled out to the hearse on a gurney so she could be taken to the funeral home. *Was this real?* I now had the responsibility to call my kids, my sisters, and my brother to tell them the bad news, and Johnny would never get to meet or know how wonderful, kind, and sweet his grandmother had been. Eileen said she would call Bonnie and tell her the news. The next few days were spent planning a wake and funeral, allowing for our sisters and brother to be able to get here in plenty of time.

I had decided I was going to stay on for a few months after the funeral to help get my mother's house ready to be sold. It needed some simple cosmetic things done to it, which I could easily take care of myself. I couldn't believe how many friends my mother had made during the years, and I was surprised to see many of my school chums attending the service. There were just two people I had wished could have attended, Johnny and Scott. Johnny took over for Frank's business, and Scott's mother had been rushed to the hospital with a high fever, which thankfully turned out only to be the flu. I knew it was best for Scott to stay with his mother because if something had happened while being here, he would regret it the rest of his life like I am going to do. Surprisingly, I do miss Scott just as I miss Johnny. I am sure we will talk on the phone from time to time.

There is just one thing (*a silver lining perhaps?*) in all this sadness; it was the first time in over twenty years all eight of us had been together at once. Life *is* strange. When I had gone to visit my mother at her grave, I made sure I thanked her for bringing us all together for the first time in many years. I am sure she was looking down, nodding, and maybe thinking that she wished it had been under more happy circumstances. I smiled at that thought.

Within a few months, the house was about ready to be put up for sale—I anticipated a quick sale. The outside had a fresh coat of paint, and all the rooms on the inside had been repainted to give the place a new look. I only had the floor in my mother's bedroom left to have refinished because it was grossly worn out, and that was going to be done next week by one of Danny's friends. After the house sold, I would head back home, but I wasn't sure where that was anymore. If it wasn't for Johnny and my grandchild, I might have stayed and bought the house for myself, but there was no way I was going to miss spending time with them because I wanted to watch my granddaughter grow up. There had been way too much time wasted already!

As I suspected, it only took about two weeks to sell the house. A nice family with two children was going to buy it. I was thrilled, but now came the hard part. We only had a month to clean everything out of the house. No one wanted any of the things, except for a few items, and those were for sentimental reasons because everyone had homes and their own things, which they had accumulated over the years. Bonnie had come one weekend to help me go through our mother's personal things, and we put the furniture up for sale. My mum had a lot of really nice things, and they sold quickly. There was a hope chest, however, that had belonged to our great-grandmother, which I wanted in the worst way. I finally decided I would pay the exorbitant price to have it shipped to Fiona's, where it would be stored until I could get a place of my own.

On the day I was to leave to go home, I was sitting on one of my suitcases waiting for my taxi to come to take me to the airport when there was a knock on the door. I thought that was strange because taxi drivers don't usually come to the door. Maybe it was Eileen coming to give me a final goodbye, which was odd because I had just seen them all last night when they took me out to dinner.

"Come in!" I shouted.

The door opened slowly, and as I looked up, I saw him. "Scott?"

"Does someone need a ride?" he asked standing just by the door smiling.

I stood and ran right into his arms. It felt so good. "What are you doing here?" I asked him just as he kissed me tenderly on my mouth.

"I've come to take you home with me, and I won't take no for an answer!" I squeezed him so tightly, I thought he would break in two.

"I was just thinking of you, of us. I know you love me, and I know I love you." I said with tears trickling down my cheeks. "I *do* love you, and I have never stopped," I repeated to him.

We kissed again, he turned and grabbed my luggage and out the door we went to our waiting taxi.

THE END

EPILOGUE

One year later
I had taken a trip to New England to visit with my sisters and to meet Rose's new boyfriend whom she told me was *the one!* I was happy for her because she had worked so hard at making her business succeed and finished her schooling that she had neglected to have a social life.

Where had the time gone? It was while I was visiting them, I decided to drive by Jack's house and to stop in to see Joanne, my old friend. The neighborhood looked the same, and Jack's house was still empty. There was a car in Joanne's yard, so I assumed she was home. She was excited to see me and asked me if I came back for Jack's funeral. I looked at her strangely.

"No, I came back to visit Rose and my sisters," I explained. "Jack died?" I was shocked.

"Yes, two days ago; Bill discovered him when he went over to visit. Jack hadn't been well for about a year, and several months ago, he came back to the house to live; Bill found him lying in his bed. He must have died in the night. When he had first returned, he was definitely a different person. He never went out, and no one came to visit him that I saw, except Bill. Jack became a bit of a recluse." she explained.

I think she was waiting for me to feel sad, but I felt *nothing.* After all the things he had done to me, it was hard to feel sorry for him. *He got what he deserved!* "Do you know how he died?" I asked her out of curiosity.

"Bill said he had pancreatic cancer, and Jack hadn't been very open with the details, even with Bill. Did you notice the for-sale sign in front of the house? Bill told me Jack was selling it because he had planned to go live out his remaining time with his son and his wife. He hardly ever saw them, and apparently, his son now won't be going to the service because his wife is ill. Such a sad family."

I asked her if she had the particulars on the service. She remarked that he was going to be cremated and the service would be in two days. Joanne wrote out the address of the funeral home and then added, it was Bill who wanted to give him a service of some kind. *Maybe I will go. I would like to see Bill because he was such a nice man.*

I did end up going to the service. I wanted to say hello to Bill; he was Jack's one and only true friend. When I had walked in, there were some flowers and a picture of Jack in a nice frame with candles around it set on a pedestal. None of Jack's family were there, at least, not anyone I recognized. I scanned the room, and I spotted Bill sitting with his lovely wife. I walked over to them to offer my condolences. Bill was surprised to see me there because he knew everything that had happened between Jack and me.

We chatted for a little bit, and I explained how I learned of Jack's death, and I was back living in Florida. I mentioned I came to visit my daughter and sisters, who were still living here in the area. He told me he and his wife were grandparents, which took up a lot of their time because of babysitting, but they loved it. After about a half-hour of catching up, we said our goodbyes, and I left.

Outside in the fresh air, I took in a deep breath through my nose and slowly let out a big sigh—another horrible chapter in my life was finally over. I glanced at my watch and realized that I had to hurry to Rose's home, as she was hosting a sort of birthday party for me. I chuckled about it because I don't really celebrate birthdays, but I suppose we can celebrate the beginning of a *new* chapter in my life. I will be going back to school to get my law degree, and the man I love more than anything is waiting in Florida to *remarry* me in a few weeks, but the greatest gift of all will be Johnny and his family attending my wedding—I can't wait to get back home.

ABOUT THE AUTHOR

Ms. Bogacho lives in a small town in New England. She is married and has two children and three grandchildren. Since she was twelve years old, she had been interested in writing and wrote many short stories for her classmates.

After she was married, she had to put her writing on hold while working full time and raising two children. During those busy years of going to soccer games, basketball games—doing all the parent things—her dreams of writing were forgotten.

After retiring a few years back, she discovered that she had a lot of free time on her hands and quickly realized that time was now on her side to make her dream of writing a novel come true.